Sage Country Book Two

ALTA VISTA

By DAN ARNOLD

SAGE COUNTRY

Book Two

ALTA VISTA

©

By Dan Arnold

Edited by:
Ellenor Wiley Clyde Welch
Cover design: Dan Arnold
Photo credit: Dan Arnold

ALTA VISTA

1.

With two short and one long blast of the whistle, the Union Pacific train from Denver to Cheyenne chugged to its usual stop at Bear Creek, Colorado.

It was the third time I'd arrived there by train, but it wasn't the first time I'd ever been met at this railroad depot by a beautiful woman. She was wearing a dress she knew would please me. It was emerald green satin with long sleeves, the one with silver piping trim on the collar, cuffs, and as a border along the bottom hem. The bustle made it stylish. Her hat was of matching color and style with a spray of golden plumes, set at an angle on her head. Kidskin gloves in a golden color completed the outfit. She was easily the most beautiful woman in Bear Creek, probably in all of Colorado, maybe even the whole world.

This wasn't just any beautiful woman either. She was my fiancée, Lora O'Malley. Mrs. O'Malley to be more correct, or the widow O'Malley, some might say. Her husband of many years had died, leaving her alone with no children and a big empty house. Eventually, to make ends meet, she'd been forced to turn her home into a boarding house. She'd made a success of it, in part because she was so beautiful and gracious, she was a renowned cook, and Bear Creek was a boom town.

"Oh, John, thank God you're home!" Lora cried, as she rushed into my arms.

I dropped my gear on the platform. I knew it was unseemly, perhaps even vulgar, but I kissed her right there in front of everyone at the station. It was becoming a tradition—a tradition I hoped to enjoy for the rest of my life.

"I missed you so, darling," she whispered in my ear.

I held her at arm's length and looked into her deep brown eyes. "I couldn't stay away from you for one more minute." I said.

"How was California? You'll have to tell me everything."

Gathering up my saddle bags and my valise, I took Lora's arm and we walked down the stairs and off the platform. I tucked my valise and my saddle bags into the back of the Phaeton cab, then helped Lora step up inside.

Taxi cabs were now the preferred form of travel for arriving train passengers in Bear Creek. The nearest hotel was four blocks away and up-hill from the train depot, and the weather could be challenging at almost any time of year. This Phaeton was kind of a luxury. Lora had secured the services of the cabbie to drive her to the station and both of us back to her house on the far western side of town. Lora had a fine carriage and two beautiful horses to pull it, but she was not skilled at harnessing or driving them.

***

I smiled as I observed several fashionably dressed people walking on the new sidewalk bordering the newly bricked street.

When I had first come to Bear Creek, only a year or so ago, the streets had been dirt and they turned to mud every time it rained. There had been no sidewalks, just boardwalks, and those only in front of the businesses surrounding the square.

We were becoming quite the sophisticated metropolis. Now, thanks to the catalogue companies and the railroad, folks in Bear Creek were as well dressed as people in Boston, Chicago, or New York.

Alta Vista County boasted nearly ten thousand people now, and about half of those lived in and around Bear Creek.

Bear Creek was the center of a cross roads for mining, farming, ranching, railroad, banking and shipping. The town had a school through grade twelve, with four teachers. The streets were being bricked and there was talk of a college coming to town. Signs of modern life could be seen everywhere. There were even plans to bring electric lights and telephone lines from Denver.

But like any boom town in the late 19th century, Bear Creek had its share of problems.

I was the new Sheriff of Alta Vista County, having been elected only a few months before. The sitting sheriff had resigned under charges of incompetence and possible involvement in the theft of a mine payroll.

Two of his deputies had stolen the payroll in collusion with a third man named Ed Rawlins. Rawlins was a hired killer who had fallen on desperate times. I ended his career one day in the street outside the Bon Ton Café.

That shooting, along with newspaper stories suggesting I'd killed the two payroll thieves at their camp in the mountains, had made me famous, and advanced my reputation as a lawman that killed without hesitation. I didn't like any of it, not at all.

Because I was living in the dormitory in the basement of the big, new, granite courthouse on the square, we only had a few blocks to ride before we stopped to drop off my gear on the way to Lora's house.

"I brought you a wedding gift," I said, giving her a squeeze.

"Really, what is it?"

"You'll just have to wait till the wedding, to find out. How are the plans coming along?"

"All ready to go. Oh, guess what, we've got a new preacher!"

"Really, do we need a new one?"

"Yes, Bud and Mildred were called away. There was some sort of family emergency back east. Bud sent for this new gentleman, and introduced him last Sunday morning."

"Okay, what's he like?"

We were approaching the square. I noticed the Palace was all lit up with those new electric light bulbs. The lights were battery powered. The batteries came by train from a place in Cheyenne. It was one of the reasons the Palace was the best known restaurant and saloon in all of Colorado.

Lora turned to face me. She studied my face for a moment. "He's a little older, but I think he's kind of like you, John."

"Is he—in what way?"

She took my arm and we leaned into each other. "He's a hard man with a hard background. You've probably heard of him."

"What's his name?"

"Wes Spradlin. Have you heard of him?"

"Yeah, I've heard of Wes Spradlin. He's a known gunman; they say a killer for hire. I never heard of him being a preacher."

The mention of Wes Spradlin got me thinking about Bob Logan. Bob was one of my deputies, a former Pinkerton detective, but he was also a hired gunman and part time bounty hunter. Bob left Bear Creek to hunt for the Thorndyke boys at about the same time that I left for California. It got me to wondering where he was now.

"That's all in the past. He went to a seminary and got his preacher credentials."

"Bob?"

"No, silly, Wes Spradlin did. Who said anything about Bob?"

The driver stopped the Phaeton at the courthouse.

"I'll be right back, Baby. I'll just drop my things inside and say hello to the boys."

"John, don't get caught up in Sheriff's business. You come right back out here."

"Yes, ma'am, I'll surely do that."

When I went into the basement of the courthouse, I saw one of the newer deputies down the hall by the jail cells and gave him a wave. I remembered his name was Shelby Matthews.

I found Buckskin Charlie holding down the fort in the downstairs office, he was sitting behind the desk. I had my "official" office upstairs in the main part of the courthouse, but the basement was where the real work got done. Charlie had become my Chief Deputy when Hugh Lomax, the best lawman I had ever known, cashed in his chips about a month back.

Buckskin Charlie Owens had recently been an exhibition shooter in a traveling Wild West show. He could do amazing things with a handgun or pretty much any type of long gun. He had been billed as "Buckskin Charlie Owens, the world's finest marksman and fast draw artist." These days, he seldom wore the double holsters or the fancy fringed buckskin coat which had been part of his stage persona, but most folks still thought of him as "Buckskin" Charlie. He had been well on his way to becoming a famous entertainer, until he'd gotten sick of show business.

Before the Wild West show, he was a little known and underappreciated law man. I'd been thrilled when he accepted my job invitation.

"Well, look what the cat dragged in? If it isn't John Everett Sage, in the flesh! I didn't expect to see you till tomorrow, John. I thought Lora was meeting you at the station."

I grinned. "She did, and I would remind you we won't be married till next Saturday."

"Why, sure, I know that ... I just meant... er ... I figured I would probably already be asleep when you came in."

I laughed. "Yeah, wouldn't surprise me. So, what's new?"

"Well, let's see ... we have four prisoners in overnight. If they can pay their fines, they'll go home tomorrow. They're in jail on drunk and disorderly charges. Couldn't even stay sober till sundown! We've also got two more prisoners awaiting trial, one for armed robbery, and one for attempted murder."

I whistled. "It seems to have been a lively time since I left."

"No more than usual, but the town is growing."

"These men were all arrested here, in town?"

"No, the attempted murder happened on the other side of the tracks, on the construction site for the new hotel, out by the rodeo grounds, what we're calling the fairgrounds now.

The armed robbery was on the road between here and Waller. That feller is just down on his luck and desperate. He stopped a stagecoach and robbed the driver and the passengers at gun point. We caught him the next day. He seemed almost glad to be arrested. The other feller is a construction worker who attacked one of the delivery drivers on the job site. Nearly beat him to death with a claw hammer. He said it had something to do with his wife."

"How is that attempted murder?"

"He'd already threatened the other man in front of witnesses, and he'd been telling people all over town that he intended to kill him. The delivery driver is hurt bad. He'd be dead if some of the other men out there hadn't intervened.

I nodded. "How's Tom doing?"

Tom Smith is the Chief of Police in Bear Creek. We used to be deputy town marshals together. He and his wife Becky took me in when I first came to Bear Creek, and Tom was going to stand by me as my best man at the wedding.

"Tom's busier than a one armed paper hanger. The city council has him and his 'police officers' enforcing every ordinance on the books and some that ain't in no books—not just the list of rules you left them with when you were town marshal. They have a whole long list of possible infractions, from littering to spitting on the new sidewalks."

"I guess the city council wants to generate some revenue in addition to the property taxes."

Buckskin Charlie made a disgusted face. He never was very fond of other people's rules.

"... And there's a fair amount of new crime popping up all over town."

"Really, like what?"

"John, it looks like some of the so called 'respectable' business owners are making a little money on the side from shady business in back rooms. The money is in gambling and prostitution mostly, some crooked real estate deals, right and left. There are some rough looking characters loitering around, more drunkenness, and petty crime, too. We've got some young kids stealing from the grocery store, and we even have thefts from people's homes."

"We saw it coming. A town can't swell up like this without people trying to steal other people's hard earned money, one way and another. As the Chief of Police, all of that is in Tom's bailiwick. He's responsible for the city. We'll be focusing on the crime in the rest of the county."

"Yeah, anyway that's why we have those four drunks locked up here. Tom's city jail is too full."

"Listen, Charlie, I've got to go. Lora is waiting for me outside in a cab. We'll catch up more tomorrow."

"Yeah, okay, it don't pay to keep a lady waiting. I'll look forward to hearing about California. Say 'hey' to Miss Lora for me."

Dan Arnold

2.

"So, tell me all about California," Lora said.

We were sitting in the parlor living area on the first floor of what would soon be "our house." Tonight though, it was still Mrs. O'Malley's Boarding House, and there were people in and out.

"Well, the train ride alone was something. At times, we were going about a mile a minute! In the time it takes to groom and saddle Dusty, that train might be fifteen or twenty miles down the track! I mean we might travel more than fifty miles in a single hour. That could take two days on horseback."

"My goodness, it sounds frightening!"

"Naw! It was smooth and gentle. I was on that train for two days going to San Francisco and two days coming back. It was riding in style the whole way."

"What was San Francisco like?"

"I'd say about as big as Chicago, but with a lot more hills. They have cable cars there, just like in Chicago or the system they're building in Denver, but there's the big bay on one side and the whole Pacific Ocean on the other. Chicago just has the big lake that looks like an ocean. San Francisco is a real seaport, and it's a couple of hundred years old.

You never saw such a busy place, and there are people there from all over the world.

There's a part of the city they call China Town. I expect just that one part of San Francisco is as big as Bear Creek."

"Where is your family now?"

"They were camped down the coast a ways, near a place called Carmel-by-the-Sea. It's beautiful there. The mountains come right down to the ocean. There are towering cliffs above the sea and gravelly beaches with driftwood and tide pools.

I expect they'll stay there for a while. It seems kind of funny, my people, the Romani, in a 'gypsy' camp, and right nearby there's a fancy hotel and resort called the Del Monte. It was built by some railroad tycoons. It burned down a couple of years ago, so they just rebuilt it, only bigger and better. Rich folks go there to play golf and have dances and picnics and what not."

"Wait, did you say they play gulf there? What is gulf?"

"No, I said *golf*. Golf is a game from Scotland. I think the term 'golf' comes from the letters that signify "Gentlemen Only, Ladies Forbidden. At least that's what I was told.

Basically, the game involves hitting a little ball with a stick. They call it a golf club, and the goal is to whack at the little ball with the stick and try to knock the ball into a hole in the ground. They have these holes scattered all around. The person who gets the ball into all of the different holes with the least amount of whacking wins."

"That sounds silly," Lora giggled.

I snorted. "Yeah, I don't think golf will ever catch on and become popular with the general public."

"Tell me about your family."

"Mother was thrilled to see me of course and she asked all about you. My son, Nick, and his new wife Rachel are very happy. He's taken a job helping rebuild and restore a big old Spanish mission there in Carmel. It was settled at about the same time as San Francisco, part of the Spanish chain of missions in Alta, California."

"Oh, I would love to go out there and see all that!"

"Well then, we'll just have to do it. Like I said, I expect they'll be there for some time. With that much available wealth at the Del Monte nearby, they'll camp there and make a living entertaining the rich and famous for a while. It's a good place to winter over.

You remember, I told you my mother is a fortune teller? She 'reads' other people's fortunes with tea leaves or tarot cards or her crystal ball, but somehow she never sees what's coming right at her. I worry they'll make a mistake in California like they did in New Orleans.

My people didn't realize when they set up their carnival where they did, they were stealing money from the local fortune teller who belonged to a voodoo sect, and they hadn't bought the proper 'permits' from some local merchants who controlled the law enforcement. My family ran head first into some cut throats and riff raff in New Orleans. The visit ended suddenly and so did the lives of some people."

"John, you've never told me that story. There is so little I know about your life before you came to Bear Creek. What was it like growing up as a Gypsy?"

"As you know, I wasn't really born a Romani. When I was a ten year old boy, I staggered into a circle of firelight one night. I was nearly frozen, half naked, and covered in blood. Some of that blood was my own. The people with whom I'd been living were massacred by Indians.

The campfire belonged to a group of Romani who saved my life, and, since I had no one else, they became my family. Kergi Alexiev Borostoya and his wife, Sasha, had no children, so Sasha became my mother, and Kergi became my father. We traveled thousands of miles together over the years. I learned many useful skills.

The Romani have learned from hard experience to stay on the move. Some of us are horse traders, tinkers, stage performers, circus folk, migrant workers and so on. Although a few have learned to settle down and grow roots, there has always been little love lost between my people and the people of the towns.

In the centuries of constant travel from the Near East across Europe and into the New World, the Romani have developed independent laws and customs. They're often despised by the locals who spit and call them 'damn Gypsies'. Our ways seem strange and foreign to the 'Townies'."

"I'm sorry, John, I've never met any of the Romani. I never heard the word till I met you. We all just grew up saying 'Gypsy'. I hope I didn't offend you."

"No, Lora, I'm used to it. But the truth is I'm more of a townie than a gypsy."

I was remembering the difference between being a true Romani and a townie was the thing that ruined my first marriage.

***

As we traveled the country and I grew into manhood, I found myself drawn to a beautiful girl, one of our people. Katya was my first love.

When I was twenty, I took a job in Texas in one of the towns where we'd been camped and persuaded Katya to be my wife. I tried to make a life in that town with Katya, she aimed to make it work, and for a while we were happy. We had a son we named Nicolae.

But life in a town apart from her people was not good for Katya. She became more and more heartsick and miserable.

Then, one day, while I was gone driving a herd of cattle to Cheyenne, she took our son and joined a different band of Romani who happened to be passing through. They were her people and distant relatives, so they were happy to have her, I suppose.

They'd been gone for nearly a month by the time I came home to an empty house. It took me another seventeen days to catch up with that band of travelers and when I did, Katya and Nicky were not with them. Those Romani wouldn't tell me where my wife and son had gone.

Whenever I could and whenever their travels brought them close enough, I would go home to Sasha and Kergi. Sasha always told me she had heard good things and that all was well with Katya and Nicolae, but she did not know where they were. I'd leave money with Kergi and he would see to it that their needs were met, somehow. After many years, I eventually gave up any hope of finding them and got on with my life. That life had become law enforcement, first as a deputy sheriff in Arkansas, later as a Texas Ranger, now as the Sheriff of Alta Vista County, Colorado.

***

"John, you must be very tired. You drifted off there for a little while."

"I'm sorry, Lora. I guess I am tired. Let's talk about the wedding."

3.

It was Sunday morning, and in Bear Creek, for some of us that meant going to church. People traveled into Bear Creek from miles around to come into town and attend church services.

There were five churches in town, the First Baptist, the Methodist, the Lutheran, our church, and the Catholic mission that had originally put Bear Creek on the map.

The white washed church with the tall steeple we attended could seat about a hundred and fifty folks and was always full.

On pretty days, I could just stroll over to our church. It was only about six blocks away and downhill from the courthouse, on the northwest side of town, well within walking distance of the courthouse. It was about the same distance from Lora's house, and in good weather she would walk there and meet me at the church.

The next time I'd walk to the church, I would meet her there, and we would be going home together as man and wife.

Folks tended to get to the church early on Sunday morning and stay late after the service. We often had dinner on the grounds. We gathered together at the church for various meetings and social events as well.

Today, I would meet Wes Spradlin, ostensibly the new preacher. I had known of him for years. He had a reputation as a dangerous man and a natural born killer. It was hard for me to imagine him as a preacher. I wondered what his game was.

As I approached, I could see horses and buggies tied up all around the church grounds.

There were little knots of people here and there, all decked out in their Sunday best. I knew nearly all of them. "Hey Sheriff, good to see you," "Morning Sheriff, we're sure looking forward to the wedding," and "I heard you were in California," were some of the greetings.

"John," Becky smiled, as I shook hands with Tom. "We are so glad you made it back safely." She gave me a hug.

"Thanks, me too," I replied. "Have you seen Lora?"

Becky nodded. "She was over on the other side of the church with the Courtneys a little while ago."

"The Courtneys" were William Courtney, his wife Annabelle, and their lovely daughter Lacey. Bill owned the Bar C ranch, the single biggest ranch in the county. In fact, at more than 35,000 acres, part of his ranch was over in Chaparral County. Bill had nearly been a casualty of the Chaparral County war. He was ambushed and shot by the Sheriff of Chaparral County, Joe Holden, but he survived and was doing well.

"Becky, I hear Lora's wedding dress is a work of art. She says you've outdone yourself."

"Wait till you see it, and then decide," she replied, with just a hint of smugness.

I grinned at her. "I'm looking forward to it. If you'll excuse me, I'll go find my fiancée."

***

I found Lora with the Courtneys, their ranch foreman Glen Corbett, who I knew was sweet on Lacey Courtney, and another man I didn't know.

"Bill, you look great. I'm sure glad to see you up and around. Hello, Annabelle, Lacey," I said, tipping my hat to the ladies as I took Lora's offered hand. "Howdy Glen, how are you doing?"

Bill introduced me to the stranger. "John, I'd like you to meet our new Preacher, Brother Wes Spradlin. Wes, this is John Everett Sage, the Sheriff of Alta Vista County."

I found myself looking into the grey eyes of the notorious gunman, Wes Spradlin, who was reaching out to shake my hand.

I hesitated for a moment. He noticed and smiled slightly

"I've heard of you," I said, briefly shaking his hand.

"Yes, I suppose you have, as I have heard of you," Wes Spradlin replied. "I'm looking forward to officiating at your wedding on Saturday."

I was tempted to point out that he had contributed to a lot more funerals than he had to weddings, but I restrained myself. After all, the same could certainly be said of me.

"If you folks will excuse me, it's about time to get the service started." Brother Spradlin turned and headed into the church.

As he started up the steps, people began to follow him inside. Soon the first hymn was being sung. When he got around to giving his sermon, I paid close attention.

***

"...so, you see when God is at work, there is always change. Just as He changed Moses from a Prince of Egypt into a sheepherder and changed him again into the leader of His people and the Law Giver, He changed His chosen people from slaves in Egypt into a prosperous nation. God changed David from a lowly shepherd boy into the King of Israel. He changed others from dead, back to living. He even changed Jesus, His own son to become like us in the form of a little bitty baby, born of a virgin. He changed Saul, a man whose only life goal was to see Christians persecuted, into Paul, an Apostle and one of the greatest saints in the Bible. I'm here to tell you that He changed me, and He can change you."

Wes Spradlin paused in his sermon, for a moment of reflection.

"I know some of you are aware, I was a bad man. I don't mean just another ordinary sinner like everybody else, oh no. I was hell bent. I had no respect for anyone or anything. I loved no one, not even myself. Before God got ahold of me, I would do anything for money, power, or personal pleasure. There was pretty much nothing I wouldn't do. I did whatever I wanted, whenever I wanted, and if somebody got in my way... I removed them."

Yeah, I was familiar with his history. His self-description was pretty accurate.

"But God, who is rich in mercy and loves us all more than we can imagine, had a plan for my life. He has a plan for your life too.

Listen to me now! God is all about changing people's lives. He has a plan and He wants you to experience His love and gentle leadership. He wants to heal your hurts and mend your relationships. He wants to make you a light to the world and an inspiration to the lost.

Are you lost? Do you know the God of Abraham, Isaac and Jacob? Moses didn't, until he met the Lord one day on a mountain. Paul didn't, until he met the Lord one day on the road to Damascus. I didn't, until I met the Lord one day on the road to hell.

Now, I don't want you to think that God will just come along one day and hit you in the head and drag you into His kingdom. He won't do that. He *will* invite you.

He has a plan for your life, but He won't force it on you. He's inviting you today. He's inviting you to live life to the fullest, to know Him and His love, to walk in newness and redemption. He won't force it on you. He's inviting you, pleading with you.

New life is free for the taking, but you have to reach out and accept the gift. If you deny Him and his free gift, he'll let you go on in your sin.

The Bible says 'the wages of sin is death, but the gift of God is eternal life, through Jesus Christ our Lord.' God offers it to everyone, but not many people really want it.

It *is* a *free* gift, *but you have to accept it* and *receive* it. A free gift does you no good if you never actually receive it.

Now, I know some of you are sitting there thinking that you are already saved, but if God isn't changing you, maybe that's because you don't really know Him. Maybe for some of you, today is the day; this is the moment of salvation. You have to make a decision. I've decided to follow Jesus. How about you?

Open your hymnal to page three fourteen, and sing along. I'll be waiting here if you want to come forward to tell me that you have decided to follow Jesus."

***

After the service we all had to greet Brother Spradlin on our way out the door. People mumbled "welcome, we're glad to have you, nice sermon," and so on, as they shook his hand.

Lora said "Thank you, Brother Spradlin, I've always heard when a person preaches you should 'tell us what you're gonna tell us, tell us, then tell us that you told us.' You did a fine job today."

I had to grin.

So did Wes Spradlin.

We caught each other's eye for a moment. What I saw there was a kind of deep calm, like the calm before a storm. I would have to wait and see about him.

Dan Arnold

4.

The next morning I was sitting behind my desk, talking to my deputy, Walter Edward Burnside. He didn't like to be called Walter, Walt, or Eddy. His friends call him Ed.

Ed is a young guy who had been a deputy to some very good men in a couple of towns in Texas. I had gotten to know him some when I'd been a Texas Ranger.

He'd taken a job as a railroad detective, but eventually became dissatisfied with his employers, and they with him.

After Ed got my telegram offering him a job, it had taken him two weeks to get to Bear Creek because he wouldn't ride the railroad.

"Yep, Bob got one of the Thorndyke boys over at Mrs. Poole's 'boarding house' in Chaparral County. He walked in and caught young Howard with his pants down and not another Thorndyke around. He arrested him without a shot being fired. He dragged him back here to catch the train to Denver, where I presume he turned him over to the U.S. Marshal, Maxwell Warren. That's what he said he intended to do."

"And collect the reward," I mused.

Ed shrugged. "Yep, the reward has gone up to two thousand dollars on each of 'em now."

***

The Thorndykes were a powerful ranching family in Chaparral County until they'd made an attempt to steal land and cattle and get it blamed on innocent settlers. Of course, not all of the settlers were innocent; some had been known to rustle a few cattle here and there. The Thorndykes took advantage of the situation and formed a Stockman's Association to rid the area of unwanted settlers. They hired the County Sheriff, a man named Joe Holden to be a "regulator." Holden liked to shoot people from ambush and leave a single rifle shell standing upright on a flat rock as his "calling card."

Bob and I stopped him. When Joe Holden was convicted and hanged, without giving up the names of any of his employers, the Thorndykes knew the Stockman's Association had dodged a bullet. His execution left them without an enforcer, and there were still three names on the list of people to be eliminated.

The Thorndyke boys took it upon themselves to solve the problem.

One morning, right at daybreak, they snuck up on one of the small ranches that had armed itself in defense against the killings. When one of the men in the barricaded house stepped out to get some water from the well, they attacked, laying down a hail of bullets. He was killed instantly. The others inside the house, returned fire and a pitched gun battle erupted. It turned into a siege, until the Thorndyke boys sent a burning wagon load of hay down the hill, into the house. As the occupants of the burning house staggered out of the smoke, the Thorndyke boys shot them down, one by one. In all, four men, two women and a small child were killed.

That was too much for the vigilante committee. They burned down Herman Thorndyke's house in town, with him and one of his sons, Horace Thorndyke, inside it. They were both killed. The fire raced from building to building, nearly engulfing the town of Thorndyke. Even the courthouse was burned and all the property records destroyed. The Army finally got there and restored order. The remaining four Thorndyke boys disappeared.

For their part in the violence that became known as the Chaparral County War, the four Thorndyke brothers were now wanted men. They'd killed seven people, two of whom were women, and one, a small child.

At first, The Diamond T was still owned by the Thorndykes, but the state had just seized the property.

Bud, the foreman, ran the place until it could be auctioned off.

Henry, Harvey, Howard and Homer Thorndyke, were outlaws on the run, but they were not without resources. The other members of the now defunct Chaparral County Stockman's Association considered them heroes.

It was rumored they'd inherited quite a bit of money. That inheritance was still in the Bank of Thorndyke. A bank in which they were now the majority stockholders. The bank was one of the few buildings that hadn't burned, as it was one of the few buildings in the town of Thorndyke built of brick, rather than wood.

With money in the bank, they had some freedom to operate for a while. They were desperately wicked, with time on their hands and hearts full of hatred.

A couple of the people on the vigilante committee, had been murdered since the Thorndykes were on the run. There was no way to know for certain, but everyone believed the Thorndykes had done those killings, and others.

Bob made it a personal priority to catch the Thorndyke boys.

I had too much on my own plate, to worry about them.

Eventually, Bob got too restless and, when he heard the Thorndyke boys had shown up in Chaparral County again, he came to see me.

"You do remember the terms of our agreement, right?" He asked.

I nodded. "What specifically are you referring to?"

"Well you agreed I could have the freedom to take some time off occasionally, to take a job away from Alta Vista County. I want to do that. I want to go after the Thorndykes, on my own. They are worth five hundred dollars each. I would find the additional financial resources to be of suitable motivation, even if they weren't such terrible miscreants."

I thought about it. If I said no, he could just quit and go do it anyway. He's a man hunter and predatory by nature. As long he was still technically my deputy, he might show some restraint.

"OK, but keep in mind they're wanted *alive.* There's no reward if they're dead."

It seemed that Bob had managed to catch one of them while I was gone to California.

***

"Ed, do you have any idea where Bob is now?"

"Nope, he's drifting in the wind—waiting and watching for the Thorndykes. They're looking for him too.

You should have seen him, John. You know Bob is kind of a dude, right? I mean he likes everything fancy, fancy clothes and polished boots, fancy women, fancy words, silver trappings, and all that. Well, he looked like a down in the heels drifter, maybe a down on his luck cowpoke, at first glance. It takes a trained eye to see how careful he is and how clean his guns are.

He's like you, you know, something about the way he moves and the way he searches with his eyes. Most folks wouldn't notice it, but you know what I'm talking about."

"What's your point?"

"Oh, I guess just that he could be anywhere. He'd blend in perfectly in any saloon or campfire in any little town, or even in a big city; if Bob Logan doesn't want to be noticed, he just sort of fades into the background."

"Yeah, well in his line of work it pays to be careful. If you do see or hear from him, let me know."

Ed nodded. "I expect he'll put in an appearance for the wedding."

"Why do you say that?"

"Oh, you know. It's probably going to be a pretty big social deal. There'll be pretty girls, free food and drink. Everybody who's anybody will be there. Did I mention the girls? Bob wouldn't want to miss all that." Ed winked.

I chuckled. "Yeah, you may be right."

5.

I walked over to the livery stable to check on my big buckskin horse, Dusty. I hadn't seen him for a couple of weeks. I'd briefly thought about taking him on the train to California, but I knew such a long trip in a livestock car would have been pretty rough on him. I planned to ride up to North Fork and Flapjack City in the morning, and I wanted to be sure Dusty was ready for the trip.

North Fork is nestled in a pretty little valley nearly five thousand feet above, and a little over thirteen miles west of, the city of Bear Creek. It's a steady climb, averaging a little less than five hundred feet per mile, but in some places there's a ten percent grade in the switchbacks.

Flapjack City was only about eight miles and a dozen or so switchbacks above North Fork, way up high in the mountains at an altitude of about thirteen thousand feet. It was where the miners lived and worked the mines. The mine owners wouldn't allow any women or gambling up at Flapjack City. Many of the miners had their families living down in North Fork, but North Fork was the place where all the miners from Flapjack City went for entertainment.

Until now, neither the State nor the County had any real law enforcement up in the mountains. They could do as they pleased up in North Fork. As the Sheriff of Alta Vista County, North Fork and Flapjack City were in my jurisdiction.

North Fork did have a town Sheriff named Tommy Turner, but he owned at least one of the saloons and controlled most of the "working girls."

His law enforcement duties mostly involved keeping the miners under control, by any means he felt appropriate. He would lock up the drunken miners and assess steep fines or charge exorbitant bail.

Sheriff Tommy Turner was getting rich by taking advantage of the miners, the mine owners, and anyone else he could, raking in huge profits from the open gambling—all the while collecting fees and fines from the miners and the mine owners.

Tommy had run against me for the office of Sheriff of Alta Vista County, but I won by a landslide.

The Governor asked me personally to address the problem of lawlessness, gambling, and prostitution in North Fork. He told me that since Colorado had become a state, it was imperative to bring the rule of law to the wild places.

I believed he honestly cared about establishing some law and order, but I also suspected the mine owners were getting tired of being stung with the outrageous fines and fees. I'd met a couple of those gentlemen at the Governor's mansion in Denver.

***

Dusty seemed glad to see me as he greeted me at the gate to the outdoor pen he stayed in most of the time. Maybe he just wanted the sugar lumps or dried apple I usually brought with me. It wouldn't be long now before the local apples would be ripe, and I could bring him fresh ones. I took a few minutes to groom him and work the snarls out of his mane.

I saw Alexander Granville Dorchester, III, the proprietor of the livery stable, approaching. "Hey, Al," I said; my usual greeting.

"Howdy, Sheriff, I'm glad to see you got back in time for the wedding."

"Was there ever any doubt?"

He grinned and chuckled. "Well, you wouldn't be the first groom who got cold feet."

"I believe you've met my fiancée."

"Of course I have."

I raised my eyebrows at him. He thought about it for a moment, and then he grinned and said, "Oh, good point!"

"I understand there's been an increase in petty crime and theft since I left for California. I see my saddle and all my other tack and gear are still here. Have you had any problems with theft, Al?"

"No. Not here at the stable. It looks like most of the petty theft has been from the grocery store, the general store, and people's homes—mostly from their window sills."

"That seems odd."

"Not when you consider what was stolen."

"Which was ….?"

"Food, mostly; now who steals food?"

I thought about it.

"Hungry people, I guess."

He nodded. "Brilliant deduction, Sheriff; I expect you're part way there."

He was annoying me now.

"Al, do you know who's doing the stealing?"

He looked down at the ground and scuffed his foot in the dirt.

"Maybe. Now, I don't know for sure and certain, but I figure it's the kids." He said it very quietly, almost in a whisper.

"What kids? Do you mean your kids?" I found myself whispering back.

He shook his head. "My kids are grown and gone. You come back later and we'll talk about it some more. I've got chores to do, and I figure you've got some catching up to do." With that, he walked off.

A few minutes later, as I approached the Marshal's office, I noticed a new sign above the door that simply said "Police," indicating this was now the police station. When I went inside, I found my old desk was occupied by a beefy uniformed officer with a thick black handlebar mustache and heavy mutton chop sideburns.

Seeing me, he offered a gruff greeting from behind the desk.

"Good morning, sir, how may I help you?"

"Is Tom here?"

The policeman looked at me skeptically. "Who might you be, that's asking?"

"This gentleman is John Everett Sage, the former Marshal of Bear Creek and current Sheriff of Alta Vista County," Tom said, walking in behind me.

"Saints be praised," said the policeman, blanching white and leaping to his feet. "I meant no disrespect, sir."

I held up a hand. "No, I understand; it was a fair question. You're just doing your job."

Tom was grinning.

"John, meet Thaddeus O'Rourke, lately of the St. Louis police department."

We shook hands. "It's a great honor to meet you, sir," he said pumping my hand vigorously. "I've heard of you, of course, sir."

I don't shake hands with many people, almost never with a stranger. That's why I had hesitated with Wes Spradlin. He'd understood my reluctance.

I carry my Colt .45 butt forward on my left hip, cross draw style, and I generally pull it with my right hand. I don't let too many people hold onto my right hand.

This guy was wearing out my arm.

I managed to get free of him.

"Come on in, John. You'll have to tell me about California." Tom said.

We went through the door leading into what had been my living quarters, back when I was the town Marshal. Now there was a glass panel in the door with gold lettering on it declaring it was the office of Tom Smith, the Chief of Police.

We made small talk about California and the wedding plans. Becky had finished sewing Lora's wedding dress. It seemed like everybody in the county was planning to come to the wedding, the reception or both. We had only invited a grand total of about twenty people, including all my deputies, because neither of us had any family anywhere close enough to come to the wedding. Apparently, being invited wasn't that important to some folks. They were planning to come anyway. I could see I was going to be paying for a lot more victuals and ale than I had planned for.

"Don't worry about it, John. This reception is going to be catered by both the Palace and the Bon Ton. Local folks will want to pitch in and bring desserts and what not. We've got it covered. We haven't had an occasion for a good old fashioned shindig like this for a while now."

"Okay, but speaking of food, what's this story I heard about kids stealing food here in town?"

Tom frowned. "Bear Creek has a problem with 'sage brush' orphans. Some have lost their parents to the hardships of the west; others are the unwanted children of prostitutes up at North Fork or wherever. The city has grown and so has the population of orphans. It looks like the older kids are stealing to feed themselves and the littler ones."

I rubbed my eyes. "What can we do about it?"

"Well, the churches are trying to get the county to build an orphanage. We'll have volunteers from the churches do all the cooking, cleaning, and caring for the kids, but we don't have anywhere to house them."

"How many children are we talking about?"

He shook his head. "I don't know for sure, John. No one does. It could be as many as a dozen or more."

**

I've never been fond of the term "sage brush" orphan. After all, that's how I got my name. People had referred to me as that "sage boy" for nearly as long as I could remember. The term was commonly used all over the west to refer to children who had been found alone after their parents had died or otherwise gone missing. I was one of those foundlings. I was very little when I was orphaned and I knew my name was John. I remembered that sometimes, when my mother had gotten particularly mad at me, she had scolded me and called me John Everett. I was too little to know if our last name was Everett, or if it was my middle name or what. Regardless, I was known as John Everett, the "sage boy." Eventually I became John Everett Sage. I'd been about five years old when I was taken in to be a part of an already oversized family. I was one of eleven children, living in a family that traveled a little too far into the unknown frontier.

I'd lived with them for about five years when the Indians attacked and killed everyone but me. John Everett Sage was spared and managed to stumble his way into the camp of a band of traveling Romani.

Kergi and Sasha had known me as John Sage, and, even though they adopted me as their own son, and I came to love them as my parents, I never used the name Borostoya.

To this day, whenever I hear my name I'm reminded of where I came from and curious as to whether or not I may have some unknown kinfolks somewhere. The Romani are my people, but I figure I'm also kin to every other "sage" orphan out there.

6.

I rode out early the next morning headed for North Fork. I loved this ride. The road followed Bear Creek up into the mountains. It was only about thirteen miles, but it was up hill nearly all the way. Even on Dusty, it would take me at least four hours to get there.

The city of Bear Creek is situated on a hill right at the edge of the front range of the Rocky Mountains. The railroad runs North and South. To the East, Bear Creek (for which the city is named) drops out onto the plains. As you follow Bear Creek to the West, you gradually climb first through a series of canyons between tall mesas and buttes dotted with pinon and pine, then up other canyons between towering mountains covered with pines, spruce, and aspen groves. Eventually, you come to a series of switchbacks over a low pass and get a view of North Fork, sitting in a hanging valley.

North Fork is a typical raw boned frontier town. The commercial part lines both sides of the road for about three blocks, on fairly level ground.

Businesses in town include a small stockyard attached to the livery stable, a general store owned by the mining company, a hardware store, also owned by the mining company, a post office, barbershop, stage depot, and three saloons/hotels/casinos and brothels.

Clearly, the principle reason for the existence of the town was as a service center for the miners up at Flapjack City, and the people who frequented and profited from such towns.

The primary buildings were all built of timber or logs, the older buildings warped and darkened with age. The newest ones had yellowish pine board siding with false fronts and bright paint.

The road went right through the middle of town, crossed a bridge over the north fork of Bear Creek, and continued on up the pass toward Flapjack City.

In the winter that road above North Fork was often blocked with snow for days, occasionally weeks at a time. In the spring, during the big snow melt, at the far upper end of the valley, the north fork of Bear Creek cascaded down in a beautiful series of water falls.

The homes of the residents, some of which were surprisingly large, were scattered along the edges of the meadows by the creek, and glimpsed through the trees up on the mountain sides.

At first sight, North Fork was a pretty, little town set in a spectacular location. It wasn't until you got right into town that you saw it for what it really was.

North Fork was wide open and bound for judgment. There wasn't a single church in the town. No banks or schools either. All the money went into crooked and greedy people's pockets.

I could imagine what went on in North Fork, on any given night, especially a Saturday night.

I'd seen it all before.

***

Sheriff Tommy Turner was sitting in a poker game in his saloon. The sign on the building called the place "The Jubilee House, Hotel and Saloon".

There would be no jubilation today.

The saloon was dingy and the windows didn't let in enough light, so some lamps were lit directly over the tables. Someone had made an attempt at an imitation of class with shoddy and cheap décor. However, the stink of old tobacco, spilled liquor, and sweaty bodies was completely genuine.

Even though it was the middle of the day in the middle of the week, there were a dozen men loitering around in the saloon; two at one table, five where Tommy sat, two standing at the bar, one man sitting on the stairs, and one man sleeping face down at another table. A single bartender stood behind the bar. No one sat in the "high seat" where a lookout could watch the room. None of Tommy's "working girls" were in evidence yet, this early in the day either.

Tommy, his tin star pinned to his vest, remained seated at a round table with four other men. He had his back to a corner of the room, so he saw me come through the swinging doors.

I stepped to my left so I wouldn't stay silhouetted in the doorway.

Tommy noticed and smiled with understanding.

I smiled back.

"Okay boys, I gotta go see a man about business," Tommy said, standing up. He reached down and started gathering up his money.

"Like hell you will," one of the men said. "You got thirty five dollars of my money in your hands there. You sit back down, and give us a chance to win it back."

Tommy punched the man squarely in the face. Both of the man's hands flew to his face. Blood was streaming down his chin and between his fingers. Tommy's right hand now rested on his gun butt. The other men at the table raised their hands and leaned back from the table.

"You broke my damn nose," the man spluttered, spraying bloody spittle.

"Yeah, well you're lucky I didn't break your head. Nobody tells me what I can or can't do in my own saloon. Besides, I left my ante and my bet money there in the pot. Maybe your luck will change and you'll win something."

Tommy looked over at me. "Can I buy you a drink, Sheriff Sage?"

When they heard my name every head in the room whipped around to look at me, with the exception of the man asleep with his face in a puddle of spilled liquor.

"No thanks."

"Well then, let's go back into my office so's we can palaver."

Sheriff Turner's office was just a room at the back of the saloon, behind the stairs, with a beat up old desk, a big steel safe, and another round table with six chairs. There was a door that looked to lead outside and one window with the shade drawn.

Tommy grabbed a couple of the chairs for us to sit on. He lit the lamp on the desktop.

"What brings you all the way up here, Sheriff Sage?"

"It seems you must have been expecting me. I imagine that little demonstration out there was for my benefit."

Tommy grinned. "Yep, I've been expecting you. I hear things from time to time. I heard you were planning to bring law and order to North Fork. Is that why you're here?"

"Now how could I do that, if you don't let anybody tell you what you can and can't do in your saloon?"

He chuckled. "You got that message huh? Well then, why *are* you here?"

"You got it right the first time. Tommy, this town has raised a stink all the way down to Denver. I can't and won't have gambling and prostitution, not to mention graft and corruption, openly displayed and celebrated in any town in Alta Vista County. I'm hoping you and I can come to terms on this."

Tommy Turner sat very still, staring at the floor.

"I get it. How much do you want?" he asked, looking up at me.

I sighed. "Tommy, it isn't negotiable and I'm not trying to shake you down. You can't buy me off."

"Every man has his price, Sage. Let us make you an offer."

I shook my head.

"The Governor himself has made it clear that he intends to see to it the wild days are done here in North Fork. Try buying him off."

"Wild days! What the hell does the Governor know about the wild days? I'm the one who's made it safe for the sporting girls. I put a stop to the killings and fights and stopped the crooked card games. I had the support of the mine owners. They wanted the miners back in one piece to do the work.

You can't imagine the hardship and suffering they endure up there. Some winters it will get down to twenty below. They can be snowed in for weeks. It's only natural that those men want some fun and comfort now and again. They have some money to spend, and this is where they spend it. What's so bad about that?"

"Most of that 'fun and comfort' is illegal in the State of Colorado," I said.

He was silent for a moment. Then he scowled at me.

"Look, I know you have the reputation for being a dangerous man with a gun. We all know you shot down Ed Rawlins in a straight up gunfight, but do you really think you could take on the whole town?"

"No, and I don't want to have to. Times have changed; it's time to change with them. Y'all don't have the support of the mine owners any more. I've come to you so that you can spread the word among the other

44

saloon keepers and brothel owners. I'll give you and the others thirty days to clean up this town."

He sighed. "I'll see what I can do to talk sense to the hotheads, but you're talking about stopping the flow of money. Nobody will like that."

"They wouldn't like being arrested and sent to prison either. Look, Tommy, there will still be a chance to make an honest living here. The saloons don't have to close, but there can't be any open gambling. There can't be a single casino in North Fork. The hotels don't have to close, but there can't be any open prostitution.

I'm on my way up to Flapjack City. I'm going to let them know up there that North Fork is about to change."

Tommy shook his head, then glanced at me.

"I knew this day would come, but some of the others will want to fight."

"If they want a fight they'll get it. They'll stay here all right, but I'll see them planted in boot hill."

He stared off into the distance for a moment. "You're a hard man, Sage, but I appreciate you coming to me and talking about this. Another man would have ridden in with a posse and hammered some placards all over town, giving us all notice to pull out."

"Yeah, well, I thought about doing that, but I wanted to give you the chance and the time to do the right thing. These days, there are a lot more folks here who want to see this town become a decent place to raise a family. Many of the miners are among them, and there are new settlers coming in who could turn North Fork into a healthy and thriving community.

It'll soon be the twentieth century. Here's something else to consider, there's a big timber company looking to locate somewhere near here. They might want to come right into North Fork, if it was cleaned up. They would build a mill. This town could really become something. You could be a part of it."

He nodded. "Yeah, I can see that. I know there's been talk of the wives of the miners raising a ruckus, even though some of those women are reformed whores themselves. Now they want to build a church and a schoolhouse.

It's damned hard to stop progress. I guess it's been a pretty good run, while it lasted. I'm not stupid; I've invested in some things here and there. Some of the others may not be smart enough to see what's coming. I can only speak for myself.

I know Ian McGregger will want to fight this for sure. He owns the Gold Dust Hotel and Casino. It's all he's got. Probably a couple of others will join him too."

"I'll give you thirty days; not one day more. I won't interfere or hound you between now and then, but I'll be watching. This town is going to change. It has to happen; it's going to happen, one way or another. If y'all don't do it yourselves, I'll be forced to come up here with all of my deputies and a posse and we'll clean y'all out completely and permanently."

We both stood up.

"I'll stop by to see you on my way back down from Flapjack City."

"I'd rather you didn't," he said, sullenly. "The less we see of you, the better ... for everybody."

Dan Arnold

7.

It had been a long day. I'd ridden out at sunrise to go to North Fork and Flapjack City, and I was getting back into Bear Creek well after dark. The sun goes behind the mountains early, but it had been full on nighttime for the last two or three hours. I figured it was sometime after nine o'clock by now. I'd eaten lunch in North Fork on my way up to Flapjack City, but I didn't stop there for supper on my way back. Dusty and I were both worn out, sore, and hungry. Riding downhill is hard on a horse, and I frequently dismounted, leading him down the steepest grades.

From the top of the mesa above the bridge over Bear Creek, I could see lamplight in the windows of Mrs. O'Malley's boarding house, upstairs and down. It was the last house you passed on your way out of town headed west, and the first house you came to heading into town from the west. There was a carriage house with a two seated outhouse behind it and a small barn in the pasture that went down to the creek behind the house. I wanted to stop and see Lora and maybe get a bite to eat, but it was too late to visit and Dusty needed to be fed and turned out for the night. As we passed by the picket fence in front of the house, I saw movement up on the big wrap around porch near the front door.

"John, is that you?" Lora called.

"Hey, girl," I replied, reining to a stop.

I stepped off Dusty as she ran down the steps and across the walk to meet me at the gate. She was wrapped up in a shawl, but when she got closer she dropped it around her shoulders, and I could see she had let her hair down. Her dress was light pink silk with red and blue paisley swirls. I could hear the sound of the bustle's train dragging over the pavers. I kissed her as I wrapped her in my arms.

"Oh, John, I was so worried. I've been watching for you for hours."

"Now Lora, we've talked about this. You can't keep a watch for me every time I ride out of town, and you can't worry every day about what might happen."

She looked up into my eyes. "I know, John, but tonight it's different. It's the first night there are no guests. I was all alone in this big empty house and ... you were gone, way up into the mountains, and ... well, I just got worried."

"Why sure, honey, I understand."

I hadn't thought about her being all alone that day. We'd discussed whether or not to keep taking in boarders after we were married, but we hadn't decided for sure yet. Lora didn't want to have anyone there as she prepared for the wedding. This *was* the first day in years that she'd been left all alone.

"Are you hungry? Do you want to come in and get something to eat? You can leave Dusty tied here at the rail."

Talk about tempting!

"I'm starving, but so is Dusty, and I've got to get him up to the livery stable."

"John, you could just turn him out into the pasture here with the other horses," she said coyly.

Oh boy!

"Now, you know I can't do that. They might fight, and one of them would get hurt. Besides, it wouldn't be proper."

She smiled invitingly and batted her eyes at me. "Why John, whatever are you suggesting?"

"If I turn Dusty out into the pasture, I won't be leaving here tonight." My voice had gotten husky.

"That's what I had in mind. What difference do a couple of days make?" she said.

I had to double check my convictions.

She sensed my struggle. "Easy there, cowboy, we can wait; besides, I was half teasing anyway."

"Oh, yeah? Well try that again Saturday night—after the wedding!"

"Can I at least make you a sandwich? I've got fresh bread and some beef and cheese."

"Now you're talking," I said.

She whisked away from me toward the house, so I led Dusty over to the hitching rail.

Typically, I won't tie a horse by the bridle reins. Dusty ground ties really well, but he had carried that bit in his mouth all day, so I pulled his neck rope out of my saddle bags. As I went to take off his bridle, I thought I saw the glow of a cigarette about fifty yards up the street, on the edge of the first block of homes. That, coupled with the sense that I was being watched made me uneasy. I chalked it off to being over tired and jumpy. It was probably just some gent out for an evening stroll. I started brushing road dust off me as I headed for the house.

**

"John, I really don't like being here all alone," Lora stated. "I think we need to continue to take in boarders."

"We can, but don't you think it will be better once we're married and both living here?" I responded.

She shook her head. "No, I know there will be times when you'll be gone for days on Sheriff's business. I don't want to be here all by myself."

"Are you afraid something might happen? Don't you feel safe?"

"I guess that's part of it. Having to deal with the chores and the house all alone in bad weather is part of it, but the loneliness is the biggest part."

She was right. There would be times when I would be gone. She had always had help running the boarding house. Consuela came and helped with the cooking and cleaning. The male boarders had helped with hauling firewood from the woodshed and pitching in to help with any heavy lifting.

Lora once told me, the one thing she'd wanted more than anything was a family. She had not been able to have a child in her first marriage. Her first husband's death had left her with a huge empty house and some land on both sides of the creek, and that was all. She'd taken in boarders to make ends meet, but she also thrived on the requisite activity and the social interaction with her guests. Her cooking skills had won her a loyal following, and there were days when townspeople who were not boarders were lined up to get a chance to sit at one of her dining tables.

"Okay, then. That's what we'll do. I don't want you to worry about anything. I'm sure Consuela will be ready to come back to work anyway. I would prefer it if you let her do most of the work and you became more of a woman of leisure. After all, I'm supposed to be the bread winner, and I am the Sheriff of the county. I wouldn't want folks to think I couldn't provide for my wife."

"That's just your pride talking."

"Yeah, maybe so, but I'm serious. People talk, and some of them go out of their way to find things to criticize. I am a public figure."

"And a fine figure of a man at that," she grinned.

"I'm glad you think so."

Dan Arnold

8.

It was late when I led Dusty into the livery stable to strip off his saddle and tack.

Inside, it was blacker than pitch. I lit a lantern so I could see what I was doing. I groomed him, and as I was rubbing liniment on him, I became aware of furtive movement above me in the hay loft. I was comfortable with the sounds of the horses moving about in their stalls as they checked out Dusty and me. I was familiar with the sounds of scurrying mice, and I even knew the barn owl that roosted by day in the rafters. This sound was new and unfamiliar.

I was tired of having the creeping sensation I was being watched.

The lantern cast long shadows away from us, and there were places in the stable the light couldn't reach, staying hidden in darkness. Dusty and I were clearly visible to anyone who might be watching us, but I couldn't see into the dark beyond the lamplight.

There were three ways to get into the hay loft. One way was to go up the stairs that ran along one interior wall, right by the front entrance to the stable. The stairs were there to make it easy to carry things up and down from the loft.

The second way was a ladder attached to the wall of the office going up to the edge of the loft where it became the ceiling above the office. I could see the bottom of the stairs, and I was standing near the ladder. If I attempted to climb up to the loft from here, whoever might be watching me from the darkness of the loft would have a clear shot at me in the light.

The third way up into the loft was the ladder attached to the outside of the building at the back of the barn. That ladder went directly to a door next to the big doors in the end of the loft where the block and tackle was hanging out for use in getting bales of hay and other heavy things up into the loft. There was no lock on that door, as it was at the back of the stable in the enclosed area directly behind the barn.

I untied Dusty and led him out the back of the stable and turned him out into his pen. Al had put out fresh hay for him, and his water trough was full. I went quietly up the ladder and found the door was open. I peeked into the loft.

I nearly fell backwards off the ladder when I found myself face to face with someone who had been watching me climb the ladder. I had my gun in my hand before I realized the pale face, only inches from my nose, was that of a small frightened child. It was difficult to see in the darkness of the loft here at the back of the barn, but my eyes had adjusted while I was putting Dusty into his pen. I could see the child clearly enough to recognize she was no threat to me. I holstered my gun and climbed up into the loft as the child backed slowly away from me, fear evident on her face.

"Hello there. It's okay. I'm not going to hurt you," I said. I crouched down, hoping to be less threatening. The little girl appeared to be no more than four or five years old with a smatter of freckles, straggly blonde hair with hay in it, and a dirty and tattered smock of some sort.

"Leave her alone, Mister."

The voice preceded the appearance of another child coming forward from farther back in the loft. I could see this child somewhat more clearly because the lantern down below was casting some feeble light up into the loft where he was. He was only a year or two older than the girl, with similar freckles and the same hair color. He had no shirt, and he was wearing a pair of bib overalls. He was barefoot, as was the little girl, but he had something she didn't have. He was holding an "Arkansas Toothpick," a big, long-bladed knife, trying to be menacing. I could tell he was scared, too. I could actually see him trembling, but he still managed to move up beside the girl. Brandishing the knife, he pulled his sister around behind him.

"Well howdy. Are you a friend of Al's?" I asked. "He and I are friends, too. I keep my horse, Dusty, here at the livery stable."

"Who are you?" The boy asked.

"My name is John, John Sage. I'm sorry if I woke you up. I didn't know you were here."

The boy and the girl looked at each other, both still frightened.

"Well, I've got to be going. You might want to close this door after I'm gone. Is it okay with you if I go down the stairs, so I can turn out the lantern and close the front doors?"

The boy shrugged.

"Okay, thanks. I hope I didn't scare you," I said as I walked past him. "Say 'hey' to Al for me."

When I got to the top of the stairs, I turned around.

"Oh, I told you my name—you remember—John Sage. What's your name, son?"

They were both still staring at me, wide-eyed, but the boy managed to mumble, "Jacob."

When I got to the bottom of the stairs I looked up at them where they stood side by side.

"Hey, Jacob, I'm going to turn the lantern down now and close the doors behind me, so y'all back away from the edge of the loft, and have a good night, okay?"

When I got to the lantern and started turning it down, I looked up to the edge of the loft; I couldn't see them. I went out, closed the doors and locked them with the key that Al lets me hang on to.

I stood there in the street for a moment. I was thoughtful as I walked to the courthouse where I had my own cozy bed in the basement dormitory, just down the hall from my office and the jail cells. The boy had been scared, but he had stepped up quick to protect his sister. I admired that about him.

I grinned a little.

That boy reminded me of ... Me.

9.

The gunfire could be heard all the way in the basement of the courthouse. I ran, flying up the stairs with three of my deputies, arriving on the square in time to see the aftermath.

"Bank robbery," someone yelled.

I couldn't believe it. Who would be so brave, or so unbelievably stupid, as to try to rob a bank in downtown Bear Creek, first thing in the morning?

Downtown Bear Creek was a busy place. What had started as just a dusty street with a few simple clapboard businesses was being transformed into a modern city. Nearly all the buildings were either brick or stone. The streets were even bricked now. The town had a pretty bad fire in its early years and had been rebuilt. As it grew, it was mostly built in brick and stone, bigger and better, although there were still a couple of buildings here and there off the square that were built of wood.

There were two banks in town, both of which were brick.

On the north side of Main Street, the First National Bank was in the middle of the block.

On the south side of the square, on the corner opposite from the Barbershop, was the Farmer's Bank and Trust.

I've always found that a town with more than one bank tends to be a pretty healthy place. It means there are enough people and enough businesses to support two banks. It means more available money in circulation. Bear Creek was a pretty busy place because it was the commercial center for the whole area, and the growth in this part of Colorado was almost overwhelming. Bear Creek was booming.

Criminals usually follow the money.

Evidently, the robbery had occurred at the First National Bank. I saw the tail end of a fast moving horse clattering around the corner going west on Line Street. I could hear a lot of hoof noise on the bricks and people yelling. More shots were fired from around the corner and up the street.

I sprinted for the corner with my gun in my hand, but by the time I got there, all I could see were people rushing into the street as the riders galloped away. I got glimpses of the riders as they approached the railroad tracks, but they were too far away and there were too many people in the way. I had no shot with only a handgun. I became aware of my deputies beside me. We hustled over to the bank and arrived right behind Tom and a couple of policemen.

"Back up people; make a way," Tom yelled. "Joe, you and Clyde keep the crowd back."

"Pitch in and help, boys. Ask if anybody can describe the thieves," I told my deputies.

Tom and I went inside. We found a couple of customers and all of the employees shaken up, and a dead man lying on the slate floor in a pool of his own blood. He was the only one who had actually been shot. I knelt beside him and recognized him as Ted Johansson.

He had taken a shotgun blast directly to the chest. Ted had been a mule skinner for Atwater Freight. He'd died with a pistol in his hand.

"What happened here, Dave?" Tom asked Dave Wilson, the bank manager.

"Well, Marshal, we'd just opened, and when I let the customers in, three men pushed inside right behind them. They wore dusters and had bandanas pulled up over their faces. They produced shotguns out from under their dusters, and told us to lock the front doors and put the closed sign back in the window. Two of them held guns on the customers and the tellers; the other one made me open the safe and start filling two satchels with money. They didn't even ask me to open the vault."

"How much did they take?" I asked.

"I won't know for sure until we count it, but that's the funny thing; I filled the satchels with mostly the loose and bundled smaller bills. When the satchels were full, the man told me to open the front doors again. He hadn't paid much attention to what I was putting in the satchels. They probably left about five thousand dollars in the safe, and I never opened the vault at all. They couldn't have gotten away with more than about eight or nine thousand dollars, altogether, in those two satchels. They were in a big hurry to get out of the building."

I was thinking that smaller bills were easier to pass.

"How did Ted Johansson get shot?" Tom asked.

"When the first two men got outside, Ted started to pull that gun out of his pants from under his shirt. The last man, as he was going out the door, pointed his sawed off shotgun at Ted and said, 'Don't do it, mister,' but Ted tried anyway ...."

Ted was brave, but stupid. It was stupid to try to pull a handgun against a man armed with a shotgun. Unfortunately, it turned out that Ted Johansson had been too stupid to live. Some mistakes you only get to make once.

"We heard several shots ..." I started.

"Yeah, somebody brought their horses up, and then they shot out the windows as they galloped away. We all dived for the floor."

"Could you, any of you, identify any of the men if you saw them again?" Tom asked the group.

They all shook their heads. I could see they were overwhelmed by the events of the last few minutes.

"I'll need descriptions as best you can give them. What can you tell us about them?" Tom asked.

I interrupted him. "I'm going to assemble a posse and get after them. I've got to go now, Tom."

He nodded. "Be careful. There are at least four armed men running hard and fast."

Outside, I learned from my deputies there were at least five men in the gang. Three had gone into the bank while one stayed outside the front door as a lookout. The fifth man had brought the horses up for the getaway. They'd fired several shots on the way out of Bear Creek, though no one other than Ted Johansson had been hit. The thieves rode east, across the tracks into the Mexican district, and who knows where after that.

"Charlie, there are five men we're after. I want ten men in the posse. You and Ed will be in charge. Pick seven more good men, get provisioned, and y'all meet me at the rodeo grounds. I'm not waiting. I'm going to get mounted and get after them right now."

"Don't you want to wait till we get organized?" Buckskin Charlie asked.

"I'll be on their trail in fifteen minutes; it'll take you nearly an hour to pull it all together. If you can't get seven men deputized, armed, provisioned, and ready, real fast like, y'all come on with however many you can."

***

The bricks of Line Street stopped at the railroad tracks. From here east, the dirt road went on through the part of town where most of the working folks lived. This was also the part of town where the old Catholic mission church was, and where the Mexican families lived. Going out of town on this road you would shortly come to the rodeo grounds, which we were now calling the fairgrounds, and the site of the new hotel being built.

A little more than twenty minutes after the robbery, I was following the fresh tracks of galloping horses headed east toward the fairgrounds.

Tracking is a learned skill. I learned to track from my friend Yellow Horse. Yellow Horse is half Comanche and half Cherokee. He and I worked for Charlie Goodnight down in Texas, and Yellow Horse had scouted for D Company of the Texas Rangers—my old company. I would never be able to track like Yellow Horse could, but I was better at it than most men. A fast running horse tears up the ground and leaves clear, deep impressions. Five hard running horses leave a very clear trail, even on a heavily traveled road. A child could have followed these tracks.

Line Street in Bear Creek is actually just part of the road that runs from Flapjack City, high in the mountains to the west, through Bear Creek, and then to all points eastward. It was a heavily traveled freight and stage road, as well as being the primary service road for outlying towns, ranches, and farms. It more or less followed Bear Creek out onto the plains then continued through the town of Waller on into Chaparral County where it turned south and ran all the way to the Red River, between Texas and Oklahoma.

***

I was able to lope along on Dusty and follow the tracks on the road as they ran east, until they split up. Just past the fairgrounds, two sets of tracks continued on down the road, but three peeled off and left the road. One rider going due north, the other two going southeast, and then those two split up. That was as much as I learned in the first hour of tracking, and then it was time to go back to the rodeo grounds to meet the posse.

We sat on our horses in a circle in the middle of the road near where the outlaws had split up. We all understood the danger and the difficulty of the task. Every one of the ten men there was capable and loaded for bear. We had to split up to follow the fugitives.

"Johnson, you and your men follow the trail that goes north. Scotty, you Shorty and Harrison follow the trail that heads southeast. Buckskin Charlie, you and Mulligan follow the trail that goes south. Ed and I will try to track those two hombres that stayed on the road and hope they don't split up.

My best guess is, because they didn't stop and divvy up the money, they'll all meet up at the same place eventually.

Now, y'all be careful. They'll be watching their back trail. If you get a chance to jump the man you're following, do it, but be real sure you can take him. Otherwise, follow him until he meets up with one or all of the others.

Chances are we'll all end up in the same place. It may take a couple of days, maybe more. If y'all run low on supplies, get sick or hurt, or lose the trail, just head on back to Bear Creek.

A desperate man probably won't hesitate to shoot you if he gets the chance, and he'll be watching for a posse. The first priority is that y'all come home safe and sound. Let me repeat that. One citizen has already been killed. I want each of you to stay safe and get home in one piece. If it means a thief gets away, then he gets away …Okay, any questions?"

"Sheriff, if we do get the drop on our man, what should we do with him?" Joe Johnson asked.

"Like I said before, if you do, try to take him alive so you can get him to tell you where they are supposed to meet up, and then make him take you to the rendezvous point.

If he won't or can't do that, tie him up tight, hand and foot, then drape him face down over his saddle horse and head for town. By the time you get him to Bear Creek, if he's still alive, he might change his mind about talking.

Y'all keep your eyes open. Watch where you're going and be aware of the possibility of ambush. Keep your rifles out, and be ready to use them. Good hunting, boys."

10.

Ed and I rode east on the road, with me looking for sign. With as much traffic as this road had, it wouldn't be long before the tracks of these two bank robbers were obscured. This was especially true now that they had slowed to a walk.

It can be hard to tell one set of hoof prints from another. Fortunately, their horses were shod, and I had gotten a clear look at the distinguishing characteristics. Every town had one or more blacksmiths to do whatever metal forging needed doing, and every ranch of any size had somebody to do the same thing. All of the horseshoes on these horses were hand forged and hand fitted to the individual hooves. The tracks were as clear to me as a signature.

They ran their horses for as long as they could, but they'd eventually slowed, and were walking when they passed this way.

Near the entrance to the Bar C ranch, we came upon a bowlegged man walking along with a two wheeled cart pulled by a burro, traveling west on the road. The cart was loaded with vegetables. From his cotton pants, sandals, and straw sombrero, I recognized him as a bracero. My people, the Romani, are travelers. We are horse traders, tinkers, entertainers, and circus folk. We have to learn the languages of the people in the area where we camp. I'd spent some time in Mexico and Texas, so I know a little Spanish.

"*Hola. ¿Has visto a dos hombres equitación oeste juntos? Sus caballos habrían sido caliente y aliento.*"

"*Ah, sí señor. Hace una hora, al igual que yo estaba llegando a esta carretera, estos hombres pasaron.*"

"*Bien. ¿Puede describir los caballos?*"

"*Venga, sí. Uno era una castaña con sin marcadores, el otro una bahía con una carga ganadera a su derecha delantera. Ambos fueron geldings.*"

"*Bueno. Gracias. Que tengas un buen día.*"

Ed looked at me for the translation. "I asked him if he'd seen two men, on hot, tired horses. He said he had, about an hour ago. One horse is a chestnut with no markings; the other is a bay with one white stocking on his right foreleg. They're both geldings.

That would put them about three miles ahead of where we are now, when he saw them, and we should figure to add on another three or so miles to that, for the distance they've probably traveled since he saw them. They're only about six miles ahead of us. It's interesting that they were both still together."

Ed nodded. "Did he describe the men?"

I shook my head. I hadn't bothered to ask, because I figured they'd both been wearing dusters. Those long coats would have covered them from their hats to their boots.

"They must figure we can't track them on this road, and in another hour or two, they'll be right; we won't be able to. Traffic will have messed up their tracks. You can see where even these cart tracks wipe out parts of their trail here and there." Ed said.

I could see that, but it wasn't all bad news.

"Yeah, but we have an advantage, we know they were together about three miles from here, and we have fresh horses. We might cut the distance between us a whole lot if we pick up the pace. We can travel mighty fast if we don't have to track them. Also, by now they may be going into, through, or around Waller. Maybe somebody will have noticed them. We can be in Waller in less than two hours."

We slapped spurs to our horses.

***

Waller was a little town that served as a stage stop and layover town for the freighters and folks traveling the road to and from Bear Creek. The town was named "Waller" because it was the location of an old buffalo wallow. A wallow was just a huge divot in the earth scraped out by the buffalo as they rolled in the dust and dirt. Old time plainsmen called them "buffler wallers." Waller had another distinction. It was the last town in the eastern part of Alta Vista County. In fact, the county line was right on the east side of town.

The last time I'd been to Waller, I'd been shot, and I had to kill a man. Jack Slade was a man wanted for murder and robbery in more than one state, but locally he was known as Jack Sloan. He was a two bit outlaw hiding out in Waller. He'd been hired by the mayor of Waller to act as town sheriff and protect the mayor's personal business interests.

Because I'd let Bob Logan collect the reward on Slade, everyone thought Bob had done him in. I'd been laid up with a bullet wound at the time. No one except Bob knew that I killed Slade. If Bob hadn't defied my orders and come looking for me, I would've died from the wound Slade's rifle bullet tore in me. It had been a near thing.

We found the Mayor of Waller, sitting on a chair in the shade of the porch, outside his saloon. He was a fat man wearing a blue shirt with no tie, jacket, or vest, over tan pants. He stood up to greet us as we swung down from our horses at the hitching rail. He had some leather suspenders holding his pants up, while his belly tried to push them down. I could see he wasn't armed.

"Howdy, Sheriff Sage, what brings you to our fine town?"

He knew me well enough to know I wouldn't shake hands with him.

"Mr. Wilson, this is my deputy, Walter Edward Burnside. Deputy Burnside, meet the Mayor of Waller, Mr. Spencer Wilson."

They shook hands.

"We're looking for two men, riding lathered horses. One is a chestnut, the other a bay, both geldings. They would've come through here, maybe a couple of hours ago."

"You know, Sheriff Sage, you really are a rude man. I never see you unless you're hunting someone. I'm starting to regret voting for you. Nonetheless, since my manners are better than yours, may I offer you both a drink?"

"Cut the crap. You asked me what brings me here and I told you. Have you seen these men or not?"

He was thoughtful for a moment. "Well, I don't know. There are a lot of riders, wagons, and such going through town all the time. I don't pay much attention to those just passing through. They certainly didn't come into the saloon."

"I didn't even describe them to you. How do you know they didn't come into the saloon?"

That startled him. "Oh, well ... uh ... what I mean is, I didn't see the horses you mentioned. Since you didn't describe the men, I don't have any idea whether they were here or not."

I looked at Ed. He rolled his eyes.

"Uh, huh, well, we're going to look around. I'm sure you don't mind."

"No, of course not; feel free. That offer of a drink is still open."

The tracks had finally disappeared in among all the other tracks, right on the edge of town. They'd been through Waller alright. As far as I was concerned, Mayor Wilson had just confirmed it. It only took us about thirty minutes to search the little town for their horses. I'd hoped they would have swapped horses here, but the chestnut and the bay were not to be found. An old timer said he thought that maybe he'd seen two men on horses like we described, headed east, but the men hadn't been wearing dusters.

Ed summed it up. "They may have ridden on through town, or they may have swapped horses, and their tired horses were taken out of town in a little herd of other horses. What do you think?"

"No, I think they rode right on through. I think they're in a hurry to get somewhere and they didn't want to risk getting caught here."

"They could have dropped off the money here in Waller, somewhere."

"No, I can't imagine this would be the place to meet up. It's too close to Bear Creek, and they know a posse would look for them here."

"They had enough time to divide the money, take their share and ride on, leaving the rest for the others to divvy up when they got here."

I shook my head.

"Would you agree to a plan like that? If you were a thief among thieves, would you trust someone else to leave the money for you somewhere to pick up at your leisure, after they disappeared into the unknown with whatever they thought they deserved?"

Ed shrugged, conceding the point.

"Regardless of where the money may or may not be, we have to stay on the trail of those two men if we possibly can," I said.

"If they stayed on the road, do you think we might be able to pick up their tracks somewhere on the other side of Waller,?"

I doubted it. There was an unlikely chance of that, but something else was beginning to gnaw away at the edge of my insight. It was just a vague notion, but something was starting to come into focus.

11.

Mrs. Poole's Boarding House was situated on a little hill just off the road on the east side of Waller, barely across the county line in Chaparral County. It wasn't really a boarding house. It never had been. Men came to Mrs. Poole's Boarding house to dally with the women who lived there. You could also call it a bordello, brothel, crib, or cathouse. Call it what you will. It was a whorehouse, the best known whorehouse for at least fifty miles around. That was our next stop.

I'd never ridden past there without seeing people out on the big wraparound porch. There were usually buggies and horses tied to the hitching rails at the bottom of the stairs and all the way around the two story house. From the porch there was a very clear view of the road for nearly a mile, looking east or west.

When we knocked on the door, we were greeted by the heavy set madam.

"Well now, Sheriff, I don't believe we've seen you or your deputy here before. Welcome! Make yourselves at home," the fat lady said.

Her red dyed hair was pulled up with a ribbon and she wore far too much makeup and too little clothing.

There were three other women standing around looking at us. They were in various stages of undress, as well.

Ed and I had our hats in our hands. We were all standing in the foyer at the bottom of the stairs. There were customers seated in the parlor and living room. A couple of the girls were serving them drinks.

"What'll it be, boys? ... oh dear, I can see you didn't come to play, and that means you didn't come to pay."

"No ma'am, I'm sorry. We're just passing through and wondered if maybe one of your girls or someone here might 've seen the men we're looking for."

"Hmmm, we do seem to get a lot of gentlemen callers," she winked. "And, before you ask for information about possible visitors, you need to know the only thing you can get for free under this roof is piano music, and that's only if you play it yourself! HAH, HAH, HAH!" She laughed like a mule.

I had to smile. Poor Ed was beet red. I pulled a ten dollar gold piece out of my pocket and flipped it to the fat lady. She snatched it out of the air and gave it a little bite to see if it was real.

"Ohhhh, sweetie, we could have such a good time. Why do you care about finding men when you've already found us?" All the girls giggled.

Another girl had joined the group. She was making cat's eyes at Ed.

"It's the job, ma'am. We have our duty and so few comforts. Could you help us with our inquiry?"

"Why sure, honey, but you must understand that we don't kiss and tell."

"Yes, ma'am. I doubt the men we're after would've stopped here, at least not this time. Maybe someone saw them ride on down the road."

"Wouldn't be the first time we saw the backside of a man! HAH, HAH, HAH!" Everybody was laughing—the girls, the customers, even Ed.

"This would've been two or three hours ago, maybe. Two men riding together; one had a bay horse with one stocking on the right fore leg. The other rode a chestnut horse with no markings. Did any of you folks see those men?"

"That sounds like the Thorndyke boys," the newly arrived girl said. "I saw them trotting by at about 3:30 this afternoon. I noticed their horses were kinda dirty and tired looking."

When she said that, just as casually as could be, I expect I was standing there with my mouth open.

"Excuse me, which Thorndyke boys? How did you recognize them? Have you seen them before?"

"Why sure, silly," she giggled. "It was Henry and his brother Harvey. I didn't see Homer today, though."

"You know all three of them by sight."

"Oh, I expect we know them better than that," she giggled again. "Especially Homer, he's the youngest. All three of them were here just yesterday, with two other men."

From Bear Creek, it was nearly sixty miles to the town of Thorndyke, the county seat of Chaparral County. Waller, at pretty much the mid-way point between there and Bear Creek, was a layover town for the freighters and stage passengers.

The three remaining Thorndyke boys had been part of the gang that robbed the First National Bank of Bear Creek, just after eight o'clock in the morning. They'd ridden thirty miles in less than eight hours, with Ed and me only an hour or two behind them.

The picture was real clear to me now. It was what I had been brooding on. They were running for home; they were headed for Thorndyke.

I knew where they were going, so we wouldn't have to track them. The problem was the time we'd wasted in Waller. Now, no matter how hard we traveled, they still had about a two hour lead on us. Sure their horses were tired, but so were ours, Dusty in particular. He'd carried me for over seventy miles in the last two days.

For my part, I was feeling both the miles and the years. I'd been wearing one badge or another and chasing bad men on and off for more than twenty years. I was almost too tired to care anymore, almost.

I wasn't about to forget Ted lying in a pool of his own blood, or the stolen money that people had worked hard for. The money in that safe had belonged to real people in Bear Creek, not just to the bank.

When we got to our horses, Ed had something to say.

"We're in Chaparral County now, John. We don't have many friends over here. I guess Sheriff Wilfred McCoy will help us, but I expect he'll be pretty much the only one. The Thorndykes are heroes over here."

I sighed.

"I know it. I expect they're headed for the ranch headquarters over on the other side of Thorndyke. It would be a good place to get fresh horses and meet the others. Let's hope somebody else in the posse has good luck tracking their man. We might just need their help when we get there."

It was nearly dark now. I decided to push on until we came to a good place to rest for a couple of hours. I was hoping the Thorndykes would stop for the night somewhere. If they didn't stop, they would be long gone before we ever got to Thorndyke. It was still thirty miles to what had been their ranch. It would be foolish to try to ride cross country on half dead horses in the middle of the night, but if they stuck to the road, they could mosey along slowly and be safe enough, while they put miles and travel hours between us and them. That was a risk I would have to take. Dusty needed food, water and rest. So did I. Ed and his horse didn't exactly look fresh as a daisy either. I was hoping just being in Chaparral County would make those Thorndyke boys feel over confident and safe. If they did, they would rest for a while, too.

About thirty minutes later we came to a spot on the side of the road often used as a camp ground by freighters and folks who wouldn't, or couldn't, pay to stay in a hotel in Waller. There was a little creek called Camp Creek spilling through a grove of cottonwoods and willows. There'd once been a house, part dugout and part sod, now fallen down and nearly melted away by time and weather. The freighters and others had maintained the outhouse as a public convenience, and there was a lean-to barn that offered some shelter in bad weather. Tonight, there was just one big freight wagon camped there, with six mules picketed between some trees. The driver had a fire going, and we hailed him from the road.

"Hello, the camp. This is Sheriff John Everett Sage and Deputy Ed Burnside, can we talk to you for a minute?"

"Come on in and have you some coffee," the man called back.

He picked up a shotgun, just as a precaution. When we led our horses into the firelight, the man lowered his shotgun. His face was nearly covered with a grizzled beard, and the hair sticking out from under his battered hat looked like twisted strands of gray wire. I recognized him as one of Clay Atwater's men. No surprise there, the dusty and faded lettering on the side of the wagon was visible now. It said "Atwater Freight Lines."

"Welcome Sheriff Sage, Deputy. Get you some coffee."

"Thanks, sure do appreciate it. We just need to feed and water our horses and let them rest for a spell."

"I'll take the horses Sheriff," Ed said. I handed him the reins and pulled some things out of my saddle bags, then he led the horses off toward the creek.

The man held up the coffee pot. "Name's Chandler, Zach Chandler. I see you brought your own cup."

He poured coffee into my cup, and I eased down next to the fire.

"If you don't mind my say so, you look plumb wore out." Zach Chandler said.

I nodded and sipped the strong black coffee.

"You might need you some whiskey in that coffee," he said, rummaging around in a gunny sack.

Before I could reply, he offered a bottle. "I don't generally drink it much myself, but it's a comfort to have, if'n you need it, and I expect you need it."

I let him pour a little in my cup. I held up the paper wrapped bundle I'd pulled out of my saddle bags.

"I've got some ham sandwiches in here, Zach, with some bacon and more coffee. Can I offer you some?"

"Thankee no, I've et, but you go on and dig in."

Before going to the livery stable to saddle Dusty, I'd stopped at the Bon Ton to get some quick provisions. Henri Levesque, the owner, had quickly bundled this stuff up for me, himself.

"Oh, Monsieur Sage, thees is terrible. Wees ze guns and ze, how do you say, oh, mon Dieu, weel it nevare stop?" Henri made it sound like he was trying to talk with a mouth full of grapes, what with "tar ee bluh" and what not, but I knew what he meant.

When I had the sandwiches out, Ed came back to the fire. "I watered the horses and loosened their cinches; I've got them hobbled and turned out on some grass over yonder. Do you want me to unsaddle them?"

"Maybe later, get you some coffee and a sandwich."

We sipped coffee and ate, while Zach busied himself with little chores around the campsite.

"I brung this firewood with me, just busted up crates and stuff, mostly. I remember when you could build a fire of buffler chips, easy as pie, till the buffler ran out. Then in the open range days, there was always cow chips. Now everything's gettin' fenced off. Gotta supply yer own wood. There ain't never any tree limbs on the ground, whenever I stop here."

"Zach, you haven't asked us why we are out on the road after dark in Chaparral County."

He winked. "I expect you'll tell me if'n I'm supposed to know."

"This morning, the bank was robbed in Bear Creek; we're chasing two of the robbers."

"Which one?" he asked.

"Which one, what?"

"Which bank?"

"The First National Bank."

"Oh, that's good, my money's in the Farmer's Bank and Trust. Course, I guess that's bad for other folk, though."

Ed and I looked at each other.

"They killed a mule skinner named Ted Johanson." I said.

"Ohhhh, no! Not young Ted! I knowed that boy. He was gittin' to be one of us freighters. He has a pretty, little wife and a couple of kids."

"The men we're after might've come by here a couple of hours ago," Ed said.

Zach nodded sagely.

Ed and I looked at each other again.

"Zach, have you seen two men on tired horses come this way tonight."

Zach grinned and chuckled, "Why sure, you boys is sittin' right here at my fire."

"Did you see anybody else, other than us?"

"Oh, I see what you mean, two fellas goin' on by here. Let me think."

I rubbed my face with both hands, waiting for him to answer the question.

"Well, right when I was pulling in here, two fellas went trotting by. They gave me some hard stares too."

"Did you get a good look at their horses?"

"Naw, I was busy with my team, but I remember they sure looked wore out, just like you boys. They didn't have the sense to stop and rest though. Now I wish they had, I surely do."

We all thought about that for a while.

12.

After we ate, we unsaddled the horses so they could roll or lie down. Then we sacked out in our bed rolls. I had only planned to sleep for a couple of hours. We slept for nearly twice that long. It was about midnight by the time we got back on the road. I was concerned the two hour lead the Thorndyke's had on us was now extended to more like six or seven hours, but I'd known the risk before I went to sleep.

***

The sun had just come up when we found where they had stopped to rest. It was just a grassy patch with a little trickle of spring water running through it, about a hundred yards off the road. They'd dug out a hole with their hands, or whatever, to make a catch basin so they could water their horses. We used it for ours as well.

"It looks like they rode in here about midnight to rest. They made a cold camp, with no fire. Judging by the trampled grass, the manure, and these tracks being pretty fresh, it looks like they only pulled out about an hour ago, not more, maybe less." My hunch had paid off!

"Yeah, and they had to make do without any coffee," Ed grinned.

"It's only about ten miles to Thorndyke; we can be there in about an hour if we push our horses."

"Why wouldn't they have tried to go on the last ten miles in the dark last night?"

"You can only push so hard for so long. My guess is they and their horses were played out. Maybe they needed to get there in daylight for some reason, but they *had* ridden at least fifty miles. They'd pushed their horses hard for the whole distance, and they galloped the first five miles of their getaway. That was bold but draining. I'm guessing they were just done in."

"I know *we* were. At this point, I care nearly as much about a nice hot breakfast as I do about catching them," Ed said, stamping his feet.

It was cold that morning. The kind of cold that happens just before the sun comes up on the high prairie.

"We'll have to be pretty fortunate to get breakfast, coffee, or the bandits in Thorndyke."

***

The first stop we had to make in Thorndyke was the Sheriff's office. After we stepped off our horses, we stretched and dragged ourselves up the stairs and into his new office. It had been rebuilt after the fire, along with a few other buildings, but there was a lot of reconstruction going on. The smell of freshly sawn wood was heavy in the air and the sound of hammers and voices came every direction. Brick and stone masons were also busy.

Sheriff McCoy's eyebrows shot up when he recognized me.

"Good night! Is that you, John? You look like hell."

"Good morning, Wil. It's nice to see you, too," I grinned. "Ed, this is Wilfred McCoy, the new Sheriff of Chaparral County. Wil, meet my deputy, Ed Burnside."

They shook hands.

Wil looked at me with his eyes narrowed to slits.

"I don't suppose there's any chance that this is just a coincidence?"

"What's that, Wil?"

"Well, you riding in here looking like sixty miles of bad road, just a little while after Henry and Harvey Thorndyke did. They looked about as bad as you do."

"So, they're here in town, now?"

"No, I doubt it. They never stay in Thorndyke. They just pass on through. If they tried to stay here, they know I'd have to arrest them. Sometimes they stop at the bank though, like they did earlier this morning."

"They did what?"

"Yeah, they do it a couple of times a month. I know because every time they come into town, somebody runs and tells me. That's the only thing they ever come here for. It was their daddy's bank, you know."

"You're telling me they rode into town this morning and went straight to the bank?"

"Sure, as soon as it opened, they went in and came out about ten minutes later, and climbed back on their horses and rode east. Nobody had to tell me about it this morning, though; I saw them as I was on my way to breakfast."

"How long ago was that?

"Maybe an hour or so; you're chasing them aren't you?"

I was dumbfounded.

"Were they carrying anything when they went into the bank?"

"Yeah, the same satchels they usually carry into the bank."

"Say, Sheriff McCoy, can I have some of this coffee?" Ed asked. He was standing by the potbellied stove.

"Why sure you can, son. Use one of those cups hanging there under the shelf. Would you like some, John?"

"No thanks. I need to go over to the bank."

"You want me to come with you, John?" Ed asked.

"No, you tell Sheriff McCoy why we're here, and then be ready to ride when I get back."

***

"Sir, I am not at liberty to, nor am I in the habit of discussing the personal business of the bank's customers with anyone," the manager of the Thorndyke Bank and Trust informed me.

He was peering over the top of his glasses at me as if I were a naughty school boy.

"I don't have time to be polite about this, mister ...." I took a deep breath, and forced myself to calm down. I needed to try a different approach. "All right, I'll tell you what. I already know they were in here, so just tell me one thing. Were they making a deposit or a withdrawal?"

"I don't see how that is any of your business," he said smugly.

His smugness drained away when I pulled my pistol.

"Fine, then you're under arrest for aiding and abetting fugitives from the law. Stand up, you son of a bitch."

His eyes were almost popping out of his head. He gulped loudly. "Now, hold on. I have done no such thing. The Thorndyke's merely made an ordinary deposit, as is their custom."

"Uh huh, like maybe they've done once or twice a month or so, for the last two or three months. Does that sound about right?"

He nodded vigorously. "Yes sir."

"Well then, I'll need you to walk over to the Sheriff's office with me. I want you to tell Sheriff McCoy what you just told me."

When we reached the Sheriff's office, there was a different atmosphere. A deputy was passing out shotguns to two other deputies.

"John, Ed here told me what happened in Bear Creek. If you had telegraphed me, I would have arrested those boys the minute they rode into town." He was looking at the bank manager who was beginning to puff up again.

Wil was about half right. I could have had the advantage of rapid communication, which I had forgotten. On the other hand, I hadn't had time to go to the telegraph office and compose a telegram to be sent to every lawman in the region.

"I didn't know who robbed the bank or where they were headed. I took out after them before I even thought about the telegraph."

"Sheriff, see here, this man pulled a gun on me and threatened to arrest me. He might have shot me . . . ," the bank manager started.

"Did he now?" Wil interrupted. "In my experience John doesn't make threats, and when John needs to shoot someone, he does it right away, and they tend to stay shot. You're lucky to be alive."

"That's right, I am lucky to be alive, and I want to press charges against this man."

Wil looked over at me. "John, did you arrest this blow hard?"

I nodded. "Yes, I did."

"On what charge?"

"Aiding and abetting fugitives. We can add receipt of stolen property to that, and I'm thinking accessory to murder."

Wil nodded. "Yep, that sounds about right. Okay then, Deputy Watson, lock this slimy bastard up in a cell."

13.

Six heavily armed lawmen rode out of the town of Thorndyke on the trail of two of the Thorndyke brothers. Sheriff McCoy and three of his deputies had joined us in the hunt.

We weren't bothering to look for tracks left by Henry and Harvey, because we were pretty sure we knew where they were going. They were headed for the Thorndyke ranch known as the Diamond T, and by now they had about a two hour lead on us—yet again.

This country was covered with brush, cactus, mesquite, scrub oak, sage, and the occasional cedar thicket. From a hilltop you could see across the brush for miles, but down in it, you couldn't see much beyond about twenty feet, more or less. It was rough country to travel through and hard to work cows in as there was no room to swing a rope. This was where Bob and I had captured Joe Holden when he had tried to kill me as I rode out into the open through a dry wash.

When we got close, we stopped and led our horses off into the brush until we found a place where we could look down a long slope at the ranch that had been the Diamond T headquarters, before the state seized it.

We were hidden in the brush, uphill, and about a half a mile away. I could see why the Thorndyke boys hated to lose the ranch. A stream meandered through this little valley and wrapped around a small piece of higher ground on three sides. The ranch buildings were on that little rise, surrounded by massive cottonwood trees, sycamores, and smaller willows.

It was an ideal location. There was water and good grass in abundance. It used to belong to another, smaller ranch. That family had been bought out or driven out by the Thorndykes in their land grab. With them on the run the state owned it, an example of the changing times.

When I first came into this part of the country, all this land had belonged to the Indians. Now, the State of Colorado was going to auction it off to the highest bidder.

I used my spyglass to study the ranch buildings and stock pens. There was the usual assortment of outbuildings and barns, just as I remembered it, but everything was more run down and weathered now.

One of the pens had some horses in it, but most were empty, waiting for a time when they would be used by the new owner to sort the stock. The place appeared to be nearly deserted. A big ranch headquarters is usually a busy place, but there wasn't a single person in sight that day. Either the Thorndykes had come and gone, or they were waiting for us to ride out into the open.

***

After nearly an hour of waiting and watching, seeing nothing of interest, we concluded there was only one way to find out if Henry and Harvey were down there at the ranch headquarters. We would have to go down and search. Wil and his deputies spread out to approach the buildings from all sides, as much as the lay of the land would allow. Ed and I had started straight down the ranch road when we heard a whistle and saw a man waiving his hat from the edge of the brush. We swung over that way and found Buckskin Charlie and Mike Mulligan waiting for us.

"Howdy John, Ed . . . ," Charlie started. "We have good news and bad. The good news is we caught up to one of the robbers, a feller named Watson. The bad news is he's dead. We jumped him last night just a few miles from Thorndyke. We disarmed him, but he had a little hideout gun in his vest pocket, and he pulled it. I had to shoot him, John. I'm sorry."

"His mistake, not yours, Charlie," I replied. "How in the world did you find us?"

"He lived long enough to tell us his name and where his family was. He was able to answer a few questions. John, you won't believe this but he claimed that he was part of a gang run by the Thorndyke boys. He said that they had robbed several banks over the last several months and were putting the money into the Bank of Thorndyke."

"Yeah, I learned some of that this morning. It fits with something their ranch foreman told me the last time I was here, several months ago, right before I arrested their father. The foreman said, every now and then, all of the Thorndyke boys would ride off together for parts unknown and might be gone for days. I didn't give much thought to it at the time. Still, it doesn't answer my question. How did you find us?"

"Mulligan and I brought Watson's body on into Thorndyke. The deputy at the Sheriff's office said we had just missed you, and you were headed out here. So, we came on out. When we didn't see anyone down to the ranch there, we holed up in the brush to watch for you."

"Yeah, we've been watching quite a while ourselves. Let's ride on down there now."

As we approached the complex of pens, barns, and, outbuildings, everything was quiet and appeared abandoned. I remembered how this place was bustling with activity when I first came here, and now it was just an empty place.

Not entirely empty.

On closer examination, two of the half-dozen horses on the place were travel-stained and weary. One was a bay gelding with one white forefoot and another was a chestnut gelding with no markings. The other horses were fresh and fit.

Wil and his deputies joined us as we stopped in front of the main house. The house was nothing special, just a single story clapboard building with three or four rooms and a broad porch across the front. "Didn't see anything coming in—if they're here, they're in the house," Wil said.

"I expect they're long gone," Charlie said.

"Yeah, I expect you're right. If they were here they would have fired on us by now," I added.

A quick search of the house proved that no one was there, and no one was living there at all. The house was virtually empty, but we found where some ammunition and some provisions were being stored. This indicated the ranch was a frequent stop for the outlaws.

"I figure we ought to burn it all down." I said.

"What? No, why would you do that?" Wil asked.

"I don't want the Thorndyke boys ever coming back here again. These old buildings are run down and in poor shape. The value is in the land. The state will sell this ranch and the new owners can build on it the way they want it."

"No, I won't let you do that," Wil said. "You and your deputies need that ammunition and the coffee, beans, and canned goods. You just take all that with you."

I nodded. "Okay, it's your county. I'm just tired of those boys having the run of the land. I mean to see them stopped . . . permanently."

"I understand that, John. I promise you they won't get any peace in this county ever again. If they show up around here, they'll have to answer to the law. Their days are numbered from now on." I looked him in the eye. "I mean it, John."

I nodded again. I could see he was telling me the truth.

When we got back outside, I looked around at the quiet setting and groaned. "Well, I guess we'll have to try to pick up their trail."

"Not much point in that now, John. They left on fresh horses, and they've been gone for hours. You, your horses and your deputies are about done in," Wil said.

"Yeah, and you're getting married on Saturday," Charley said. "If I don't get you back to Bear Creek in time for the wedding, I don't like to think about what Miss Lora might do . . ."

For the first time in my life I hesitated. I'd always chased my prey till they couldn't run any farther. I'd become well known for my relentless pursuit. If Yellow Horse were here to track them with me, I would keep after the outlaws, no matter how long or how far. But he was nowhere near now, and I did have a previous commitment. It was a personal and, in some ways, more important commitment. I hated to let the Thorndykes get away, but Wil and Charley were right. There was very little chance we could have any hope of getting on their trail, much less of catching up to them.

I smiled weakly. "Well, I guess we've done all we can at this point. One bank robber dead, the money accounted for, and their crooked banker in jail."

"That and the Thorndyke brothers are running like cats with their tails on fire," Ed added.

"I don't think we should leave those spare horses here." I said.

"You boys need fresh mounts," Wil said. "Why don't you swap your saddles onto um and lead your horses back with you?"

"Now that's a good plan. We'll deprive any of the others in the gang of fresh horses and save our mounts in the process." Charley said.

I thought about it. I found the idea of riding back into Bear Creek on horses wearing the Diamond T brand of the Thorndyke ranch kind of amusing.

"I don't know if that would be quite legal," I said.

"I expect it is, and I recommend you do just that. Them horses gotta be moved somewhere. The way I see it, they're part of the robbery scheme and you can legally confiscate um and dispose of um as you see fit," Wil said.

"Whoooeee!" Charley whooped. "I like the idea of the Sheriff's department having horses for us deputies to use, so's we don't have to use our own all the time."

I nodded. I liked the idea myself. The problem would be getting the Alta Vista County commissioners to approve the expense of housing and maintaining them, just another part of the politics that was part and parcel of my job.

Dan Arnold

14.

Just after noon, having finished a fine lunch at the only sit down café in town, Charley, Mike Mulligan, Ed, and I rode out of Thorndyke under a hot sun. The café was currently housed in a platform tent as the building was under construction. The food was good, though not as good as it was at the Bon Ton, but, then again, we'd been mighty hungry. We would've eaten grease fried skunk and liked it well enough.

I'd sent telegrams to every lawman within a hundred miles, telling them to be on the lookout for the Thorndykes, and I'd sent one to Bear Creek to let the office know we were safe and headed home.

We were riding due west on horses sporting the Diamond T brand. Because we had also brought along all of the horses that had been at the Thorndyke ranch, we were ponying our own horses and one more beside us.

In panniers slung on a saddle, one of them carried the provisions we'd taken from the Diamond T. I was unhappy we were going back to Bear Creek without anything to show for the chase except some horses and supplies.

We left the corpse of the thief killed by Charley—to be buried in Thorndyke.

We'd ridden a little more than five miles when we saw riders coming up the road from the west. I was pleased to see it was the Robertson outfit. There were four riders in the group. Joe Robertson was a neighbor of Bill Courtney. Robertson's 'Rafter R' ranch lay directly to the north of Courtney's 'Bar C' ranch. Joe and two of his hands had been in Bear Creek on the morning the bank was robbed. Charley had been happy to have them join the posse as Joe was an old hand in this country, having been here from the early days when white men were new to the land and life was uncertain. He'd built his ranch from nothing and buried his wife and two sons along the way. The two hands with him were capable men as well, or Joe would never have hired them. The fourth man in the group I didn't know. When they got closer, I noticed the fourth man was bound.

After we greeted each other, Joe got straight to the point.

"We caught this feller up on Wilson's mesa. Says his name is Russel, Tom Russel. Reckon he's telling it wrong. Made up name, I expect. We followed his trail, pushing him hard that first day. A couple of hours before dark we were approaching Wilson's mesa. Just below the mesa where all that exposed rock is, he figured to give us the slip. I expect he thought anybody following him wouldn't be able to track him there. Lucky we know this country better than he does. I took a chance, thinking he would go down around the base of the mesa, sticking to that rocky ground and then swing east up into the pinõn and scrub oak. Me and the boys rode straight over the back side of the mesa and waited on the edge of the piñons. Sure enough, just after dark he came trotting right up to us, and we had the drop on him from three sides. He thought about drawing on us, but I guess he knew he couldn't get all three of us, especially with us already holding our guns on him. If he'd twitched, we would have blown him right out of his saddle. I could see he was calculating the odds. I expect he's been in many a gun fight."

I studied the man. He had a hard look to him, but the years were beginning to show, and the trip had taken some of the starch out of him. He had a heavy beard, long hair, no hat, and he was some beat up. He hung his head when he saw me looking at him.

"Joe, how did you know to bring him to Thorndyke?" I asked.

Joe Robertson grinned, and there was the look of the lobo wolf in his eyes.

"Well, somehow he got the idea we were going to hang him. Now, there ain't no decent trees around Wilson's mesa, but we were only a couple hours ride from the Rafter R. We tied his hands behind his back and took off at a pretty good clip. By the time we got to the ranch and threw a rope over the sign above the ranch gate, he was plumb glad to talk. He told us he was part of the Thorndyke gang, and they were all headed for the Thorndyke ranch where they had fresh horses and what not. We spent the night at the ranch. This morning, as we were getting mounted to ride over here, he tried to get away so he suffered a beat down. We just got on this road when we met you."

He was looking at the horses we were leading.

"Looks like you pretty much cleaned them out. What happened to the others?"

I was tempted to hang my head as well, but I didn't.

I met his eye.

"Two of the Thorndyke brothers got away. Charley and Mike here sent one of the others, a man named Watson, to meet his maker."

 When I said that, the bound outlaw's head snapped up and he swore.

"Shit! Him and me were pards. Why'd you kill him?"

"It was him or me. He saddled that bronc and couldn't make the ride." Charley said.

"Is that right; did he have a chance?"

"He did—he had a hideout gun, and he pulled it on me quick like. Fortunately for me, I shoot a hell of a lot better than most folks, a little better than he did."

I knew that was true. Most gunfights are not won by speed, but shot placement. Anybody can be fast, but it's where the bullet strikes the target that counts.

Charlie is the best shot I've ever seen with a long gun or a handgun. He won't squeeze the trigger till he knows exactly where his bullet is going. That doesn't slow him down any though. He's had more practice with firearms than anybody else I know. When he was in show business, he was billed as the fastest shot in the west, which was hoopla, but he *is* much faster than most men who carry a gun. He's certainly faster than me, but then I don't fancy myself a fast draw artist.

I spoke up.

"He made his play. I guess he didn't want to hang. How about you? You knew the stakes when you bought into this game."

The man looked me in the eye and said, "At least he had a chance. Like you said, we knew the stakes when we bought in. I sure will miss him though." He looked back at Charley again. "Not many men could have beaten him once he had a gun in his hand. You and me have unfinished business."

Charley nodded.

"Maybe, but I don't think so. I think you're done. The days of settling things with gunfire are over. Still, if you get the chance, you go ahead and take it."

There was sweat in my eyes and I was irritated, so I interrupted.

"Mr. Russel, was it you who killed the man in the bank."

He shook his head.

"I don't know for sure who done it. Snooker, that was what Jim Ed Watson went by. . . Anyway, Snooker had the horses and I was watching the town from the front of the bank. When I heard the shot, I think the Thorndykes were already out of the bank. I didn't see anybody shot and didn't even know about it till these boys told me they were going to hang me for it."

I was pretty sure it was the truth. He told it straight out and didn't lie about any part of it; that I could see.

I looked over at Joe Robertson.

"We rounded up the crooked banker in Thorndyke. The money they stole is in his bank and will be recovered. The Thorndykes are running, and they're running out of holes to hide in. We're heading back to Alta Vista County, and we'll take this man, Russel here, back for trial. Joe, y'all have done a fine job. I can't thank you enough. Will you come back to Bear Creek with us?"

He shook his head.

"Nope, he's all yours. Glad we could help out. It was just his bad luck he drifted over onto our home range with us hot on his heels. We'll be heading back to the Rafter R now."

We rode west from there on the road, in a more or less constant cloud of dust. I was wondering what had happened to the men who rode off south, tracking the fifth holdup man.

We spent that night camped out in a barn in Waller. I wanted to keep a low profile, and I hated to pay Spencer Wilson even one penny for a night's stay in his flea trap hotel. We left his town at the crack of dawn, and rode into Bear Creek six hours later, at high noon on Friday.

We were a rough looking bunch of men as we rode into town. We'd had no bathing or shaving on the road, and we were covered with dust and travel stains.

The people on the streets and in the stores and what not, turned out to watch us ride up to the courthouse. They all appeared clean, polished, and sophisticated compared to us.

As we dismounted and stretched, the photographer from the Bear Creek Banner came running up carrying his big, new camera. I wasn't about to stop and pose for a picture, so I hustled our prisoner into the jail.

Charley, Ed, and Mike Mulligan did pose though. They were photographed, standing by the horses, on the brick street with the courthouse in the background. The news photographer had them stand side by side with their weapons clearly evident; each of them was holding a rifle. They were a dirty, grim, and rough looking group of deputies. Charley, with his walrus mustache, and all three with their hats tilted back so you could see their white foreheads above their dirty and sunburned faces. I'll bet everyone has seen that picture.

Once in the jail, I learned Scotty, Shorty, and Jack Harrison had lost their man. The deputies had followed the trail southeast; eventually they stopped for the night and had trouble finding fresh sign when they tried to pick up the trail the next day. Evidently the rider had doubled back and passed them in the night. What trail they found led them right back to the road. They thought the outlaw might've come right back into Bear Creek.

I thought about that.

Who was the man? Why would he come back to town? Only one of the outlaws was unaccounted for.

He'd not been seen at all. Was it possible that Homer Thorndyke could now be hiding out somewhere right under my nose in Bear Creek?

***

Later in the day I got a shave and a haircut in preparation for the wedding. All the local talk was about either the robbery or the wedding. It seemed like the wedding was the bigger story.

That evening Lora and I were sitting out on the back porch watching the stars come out.

"Consuela agreed to come back to work. I'll start interviewing prospective boarders on Monday," she said.

Lora was trying not to show the strain of worry she had experienced over the last week. My being gone almost the whole time I'd been back from California must've been really hard on her. It was hard to believe tomorrow would be our wedding day.

"Sounds good," I said.

"What is it, John? You seem distracted. Are you worried about something? It isn't the wedding is it? Do you still want to marry me?"

"Oh baby, I'm sorry! Of course I want to marry you. Tomorrow will be a wonderful day! You're right though, I am a little distracted, and I have something to ask you. It might not be right. I mean . . . you might not . . . ."

"What is it, John? You can ask me anything, you know that."

I looked down at the toes of my boots for a moment, gathering my thoughts.

"Have you heard about the children running loose in town? There's been some stealing and what not."

She nodded.

"Yes, I have. The church is forming a committee to discuss ways we can help. I plan to join in. Why do you ask?"

"Well, you see, there are these two little kids living in the hay loft at Al's livery stable. They've been there for more than a week.

When I went by there, earlier today, I talked to Al. He's worried something bad will happen to them or to the barn. It would be pretty easy for a lantern to get knocked over or something like that. A horse could kick, or . . . what if one of them falls out of the loft?"

"Oh, John! That's awful. How little are they?"

"The little boy; his name is Jacob. I guess he's six or seven. I don't know his little sister's name, but she's only four or five. Al would move them down into the room at the back of the barn, but it wouldn't really be any safer, and winter is coming on."

Lora's eyes became huge and she pulled away from me.

"John Everett Sage! How could you leave those children there like that?" she cried. "You go hitch up the team. We'll go get them right this minute,"

"Okay, but then what? What will we do with them? Where will we take them? Tomorrow is our wedding day. We don't even know anything about them!"

"We know enough. Good grief! *Men*! You haven't got the sense God gave a chipmunk!"

Dan Arnold

15.

We drove up the hill into town and parked the carriage in front of the livery stable.

I helped Lora down and unlocked the barn door. I barely got it open before she whisked inside. Not that it did her any good because it was pitch dark in there.

"Hang on a second, baby; I'll light a lantern."

When the lantern was lit, I could see the eagerness and concern on her face as she looked up at the hayloft.

"Better let me go up first. We don't want to scare them. I've spoken with them some and brought them some food and candy, so they know me a little," I whispered.

She nodded in reply.

I left her with the lantern, as I went up the stairs.

Right at the top of the stairs, I found Jacob and his sister staring at me with wide, but sleepy, eyes.

"Jacob, I'd like you to meet a beautiful and wonderful lady. Her name is Lora, and she and I are going to be married tomorrow. Would you like to meet her?"

Jacob looked at his sister, and she nodded tentatively. Jacob looked at me and shrugged.

I could hear Lora coming up the stairs, and the lantern light soon filled the loft.

I watched the children's faces when they saw Lora.

They were in awe.

So was I.

Lora has the kind of beauty some women are born with. The balance of physical characteristics which are sometimes stunning, attractive, alluring, seductive, or even inspiring to those who observe them. But that kind of beauty is only to the eyes. It's a beauty that fades with time, can be lost to trauma, or polluted by excess.

There's another kind of beauty that shines right through the physical and doesn't fade with time. A beauty more precious and rare. It's a beauty that can, and often does, increase with time. The beauty of the soul

It was this more important and rare beauty which instantly attracted the children to her, especially the little girl.

"Hi, sweet girl, what's your name?" Lora asked her.

The little girl started twisting, swinging around back and forth. Shyly she answered, "Sarah."

Lora turned her smile upon the boy.

"Hello, I'll bet you're Jacob, right?"

The boy nodded.

"Yes ma'am. I'm pleased to meet you."

See, right there, that's what I'm always talking about. One minute with them and she had Sarah's name. I couldn't get it out of either one of them. I was lucky to get even a mumbled word from Jacob, any of the times I had tried to talk to them, but she had them both talking with just her smile.

And who would have guessed Jacob had good manners?

Lora sat on a hay bale and reached out to Sarah. To my surprise the little girl walked right into her arms! Lora pulled her onto her lap, gently cuddling her. She reached a hand out to Jacob and he went to her as well.

Lora looked up at me with a look I'd never seen before.

I felt like an intruder in a place of sacred wonder. That hay loft had just become a glorious cathedral. It was as if I found myself standing on hallowed ground.

I guess I had just a little bit of insight into how old Joseph must have felt, looking down at Mary in that stable, on that day in far off Bethlehem, so very long ago.

"How would you children like to come back to my house and have some cookies and milk? I live in a great big house on the edge of town, right down by the creek," Lora offered.

Jacob shrugged again, but Sarah smiled real big and nodded her head vigorously.

***

Within a couple of hours, Lora managed to get those kids bathed and bundled into a bed in one of the guest rooms. I stood in the door and listened as she sang them to sleep.

That's how Lora and I came to have children— before we were even married.

Dan Arnold

16.

Saturday morning found Tom, Becky, and I having breakfast at the Bon Ton, as was our habit on Saturday morning, except Lora wasn't with us.

She was a very busy lady, what with taking care of the kids and it being our wedding day and all. Consuela had agreed to help with all of that.

"Well, if you gentlemen will excuse me," Becky said. "I'm tired of all this political talk. I want to see those kids, and, as I *am* Lora's matron of honor, I have certain duties to attend to. I'll see you at the wedding. Do try to get to the church on time."

Tom and I both stood up as she rose from the table and swept out of the room. I noted that Becky's pregnancy was beginning to show.

When we were seated again, Tom picked up where he'd left off.

"As I was saying, John, if having to wear a uniform wasn't bad enough, they want to rename the town. They say Bear Creek is too 'provincial' and doesn't represent the modern metropolitan city in which we live."

I chuckled at the idea. "Well I'm afraid the names St. Louis, San Francisco, Chicago, New York, and even Carson City are all taken. What do they have in mind?"

"There's a lot of discussion, but so far the original name for Bear Creek, Rio Oso, is possible, then

Middleton, Stockton, and Grandville seem to be the most popular picks with that crowd."

"Oh! Well then, I like Grandville!" I laughed.

"Yeah, that's fine, you go on and laugh, but they're serious about this."

Just then a newspaper boy came in the door.

"Paper! Get your newspaper," he called.

Tom waived him over and gave him a nickel in exchange for the latest offering from the Bear Creek Banner.

His face grew dark as he scanned the headline.

"What is it?" I asked.

He shook his head and handed me the paper. The headline jumped at me.

"*FAMOUS LAWMAN FAILS.*"

There was the picture of the deputies, right under the headline.

The story went on to say: *"Sheriff John Everett Sage and nine deputies were only able to account for two of the five bandits that robbed the First National Bank of Bear Creek in broad daylight; a robbery in which an area man named Ted Johanson, bravely risked his life and lost it at the hands of the desperados. The Sheriff failed to return the stolen money and has killed one of the outlaws, while threatening to lynch the other.*

A source informs us, Sheriff Sage and his posse has also stolen several horses from an area ranch.

This is typical behavior for the violent and primitive lawman whose history is filled with gun play.

When asked for comment, Sheriff Sage refused.

TIME FOR A CHANGE?

Surely in these modern times more sophisticated law enforcement techniques should be employed. Isn't it time for better educated and skilled law enforcement in Alta Vista County?

Sheriff Sage failed to take advantage of the telegraph system or the railroad, and decided to rely on the things he knows best, horses and guns.

The result ?

Two men are dead, and the worst offenders have escaped!"

"How do you like that?" Tom asked.

"Well, I'm not even in the photograph. They spelled Ted's name wrong, with only one 's' instead of two, and I don't know how the railroad could've been of any use. Other than those things, it's about the way it went," I sighed.

"No, it ain't! You identified the Thorndykes and tied them to several bank robberies. You found all the money they stole. You arrested the bank officer who was in cahoots with the gang. Your posse captured one of the bandits and dropped another when he attempted to kill one of your deputies, without a single deputy being injured or killed. Not to mention shutting down their hideout. You don't have to take this, John!"

"I guess it is all a matter of perspective."

"Bullshit!" Tom cursed. "It was you and your deputies, out there risking life and limb in a heated pursuit, who got all that done. If you had simply sent telegrams and waited for responses . . . ahhh, how stupid can they be?"

I smiled, remembering, at about this time last year, Tom had barely been able to read a newspaper. He'd come a long way.

"Let's talk about something else," I suggested.

He blinked at me; then he grinned.

"You're right. Today is your wedding day. I'm your best man. What a whoop tee do! Are you ready?"

I thought about it for a second.

I'd been a wandering man. After today, the only place I was going to wander was back home after work. And there it was . . . home. I realized that from now on, home was where Lora was, maybe Lora and those two kids.

"You bet I'm ready!" I grinned.

"Well then, the wedding is at four o'clock. Till then, we've both got some work to do. How about I meet you at your office at about three o'clock? We'll put on our wedding duds and walk over to the church together."

"Good plan, but I figure we'd both better be ready by three o'clock and head over there about then. I'd much rather be early than late."

"That's all right by me."

"I'll get dressed and meet you at the police station at three, and then we can walk over to the church together."

"Okay, I'll see you then," he said.

We both stood up to leave.

"And, John . . . Don't let that newspaper story upset you. You're the best lawman I know."

"Thanks, Tom. We both do our best. I guess it'll have to be good enough. I'll see you at three."

Dan Arnold

17.

When I walked into the office at about 8:30, there was a woman waiting to see me. "Sheriff Sage, I don't believe we've met. I'm Emma Poole."

She extended her hand, and I accepted it, removing my hat.

She was, like my mother, an older woman of indeterminate age. She was very fashionably dressed and carried a folded parasol, as was the current fashion, to provide shade from the sun. Her hair was tucked up under a fancy hat. The hair I could see was now mostly grey, yet her sparkling blue eyes had not faded, and her face showed few lines. She wore a small amount of tasteful makeup, and her figure was still remarkable, no doubt enhanced by a tight fitting corset.

"How do you do, Mrs. Poole?" I said.

"Ah, so you've heard of me."

"Yes, ma'am, and I've seen you about town on occasion. Please have a seat. What can I do for you today?"

She sat in the offered chair in front of my desk, as I hung my hat on the coat rack and returned to sit behind my desk.

I'd heard the famous Mrs. Poole was retired from the prostitution business, after selling out to Spencer Wilson, the Mayor of Waller, and now lived in a modest house just a couple of blocks south of the square.

It was rumored she was a canny business woman who had made quite a bit of money, both as a madam and as a working girl before that. I knew she had invested in some of the local businesses and had contributed to charitable causes on occasion. She was a respected member of the community, although her reputation made her unpopular with the local socialites.

"I've come about the children," she said.

"What children are you referring to, ma'am?"

I was pretty sure if she had any children, they would be long since grown and gone. I hoped she wasn't referring to Jacob and Sarah.

She smiled and said, "I don't suppose I could get you to stop calling me ma'am. My friends all call me by name. Please call me Emma."

"Yes ma'am."

She smiled again.

"I've become aware there is a problem with orphaned children in this town. Am I correct, Sheriff?"

"Yes, ma'am, recently there has been an increase in the number of homeless children here in town."

"I've seen quite a few of these kids. Some of the older ones are ganging together. I understand there's been some petty theft, and some of the local churches are attempting to get the county to address the issue."

"Yes ma'am."

"Sheriff, what, in your opinion, is the greatest impediment to getting these children off the streets?"

I appreciated her straight forward manner and her insight.

"Well, I can't speak for the county commissioners, or for the city leaders, but it appears to me as if they each tend to think the problem should be addressed by the other."

"Politics and bureaucracy!" she snorted in disgust.

"No, ma'am, that isn't really the problem, at least not entirely, and certainly not intentionally. The county and the city have established agendas and budget constraints. Building an orphanage will take time and money."

"How very diplomatic of you," she observed. "Of course I see that aspect, but in the meantime, these kids are on their own and in peril."

"Yes, ma'am, but the churches are forming a committee . . ."

"A committee, Sheriff Sage? The camel is a horse that was designed by a committee."

"Yes, ma'am, I know what you mean. Why are you bringing this inquiry to me?"

"I'm going to the Chief of Police after this. These kids are starting out on the wrong foot. Some little thefts and petty crimes now, but it will get worse as they become more desperate. Some of these kids will be, and probably are being, exploited, the little ones and the girls in particular. Something has to be done quickly, not several months from now."

She was right. She'd come to me partly because there was a law enforcement component to all this.

"Yes, ma'am, I take your point, but there is little I can do at present."

"I know you're doing some good things already. I can help, but not by being on some church committee, even if they would have me."

"It sounds like you have a plan."

"I sure do. I know you have laid down the law up in North Fork. You're forcing them to clean up the town and shut down some of the more, shall we say, 'colorful' businesses."

"Yes, ma'am, but what has one thing to do with the other?"

"I own one of those businesses. I have a big house up there on about twenty five acres of land. As it seems I shall have to close that business, I want to donate the house and the land to the county to be used as a school and orphanage."

Someone could have knocked me over with a feather!

"Mrs. Poole, that is extraordinarily generous. I must say, I'm surprised."

"Why do you say that?"

"Well, I'm given to understand some of the more prosperous business owners up there would like to see me dead. I'm costing you money, and you volunteer to give your property to the county?"

She looked me in the eye.

"I'm philosophical. The way I see it, I can be part of the problem and resist the changes, or I can be part of the solution and do some good. Some of those 'ladies of the community' used to work for me, and now they're married and wanting to see a better life for themselves and their children. I support that notion."

"Yes, ma'am, may I say you impress me greatly. I admire your attitude."

"Do you? Well I have some pretty serious provisions and reservations. This isn't something I'll do with no strings attached."

"You'll have to put it all in writing and present it to the county commissioners."

"Fine, but some of it involves you. You strike me as a man who can be trusted, and I've met far too few of those."

"What do you have in mind?"

***

After she informed me of her plans and my part to play, I offered to escort her over to the Police Station. She accepted my offer.

As we were walking down the sidewalk, she laughed.

"I've had a number of lawmen come to visit me over the years, but this is the first time I've gone to visit one of them. Two in one day! Times really are changing."

I reflected for a moment on the hardships of the west.

In the early days of western expansion, men outnumbered women by as much as ten to one. A woman alone out here, was a woman in trouble. A woman with young children and no husband was in serious trouble. If she had family, a church home, or friends, she would have some support and time to figure out what to do.

Most towns were so rawboned and rough; many women didn't have anyone to support them. They had to make a living doing what they could. Many had taken to entertaining men for a living.

Mrs. Poole was a typical example. She'd seen more than her fair share of mining camps, cow towns, and army posts.

***

Back at the office, I found a telegram had just arrived from Sheriff Jed Worthington of Kimball, Nebraska. He reported that Henry and Harvey Thorndyke had been seen in Kimball, and had ridden west toward Cheyenne where they planned to board the southbound train to Denver that morning. In Bear Creek we called it the 12:10 train to Denver. I usually arrived in Bear Creek at about that time, give or take a half hour or so.

The telegram was just telling me a tale that someone claimed to have overheard in a saloon in Nebraska, but it was a lead.

It gave me about two hours to prepare.

18.

The sound of the train whistle could be heard all over town. As the locomotive came grinding to a stop, steam swirled and the engine slowly chugged. The water flume was lowered from the tank on the other side of the tracks.

A few passengers stepped down from the train. Maybe some were coming to stay on in Bear Creek, others were just stretching their legs, stepping out of the way as several new passengers bound for Denver boarded the train.

I was leaning casually against a far corner of the ticket office, watching.

Two men stepping off the train drew my immediate attention.

Henry and Harvey Thorndyke looked especially road weary this afternoon. Each man carried saddlebags and a rifle, but that was all. Their clothes were dirty and travel stained. I could see their gun belts as well.

They looked around as if expecting trouble, but seeing none they started across the platform to head into town. They were walking in my direction.

I stepped in front of them with my head down so my hat concealed my face.

"Howdy boys, welcome to Bear Creek," I said, raising my head to look them in the eye.

They jerked to a stop, clearly ready to draw their guns.

Henry smirked at me. "You really want to do this right here on the platform?" he asked. "Someone might get hurt."

"Someone besides you," Harvey added, with a sneer.

"Maybe, but you won't ever know, because you'll be dead. Look over your shoulder."

Henry looked back at the train on his left. The nearest car was less than twenty feet away, and there were shotguns pointed at them from several of the windows.

All of the "passengers" who had boarded the train were my deputies.

Ed had been some put out he would have to actually board the train. He'd sworn to never have anything to do with a railroad ever again.

He was even more offended he was picked to pretend to be a woman. He was the only one small enough to wear the dress Becky loaned us.

Behind the outlaws, Tom stepped out of the door of the ticket office, holding his double barreled Parker shotgun on them. Henry and Harvey both looked around with a sick look on their faces.

"Put your hands up, boys. If you move a muscle or try for your guns, we'll shoot you to doll rags." I said.

Henry and Harvey slowly raised their hands. Tom and I disarmed them and put the handcuffs on.

"We didn't expect to see you at the station. Aren't you getting married today?" Harvey Thorndyke asked.

"Why, yes I am, but you're not invited," I said, giving him a shove.

***

Tom and I paraded them through town all the way to the courthouse. We'd only gone about a half of a block when we heard the train whistle, and, shortly later, the train left the station.

People swarmed around pointing and talking. It was quite a spectacle, but nobody came running from the newspaper office with a camera.

After we slammed the cell doors behind them, Tom grinned at me.

"There's only one Thorndyke on the loose now," he said. "You've managed to get all the bank robbers but one, and you captured these two hombres without a single shot being fired."

"I'm glad of that. I really didn't want to get shot on my wedding day."

"Speaking of which, I guess we'd better get ready; the wedding is supposed to start in about an hour and a half."

"Yep, you go on. I'll meet you at the police station at three o'clock just like we planned. Hey, Tom . . . thanks for backing my play."

"That is what a best man is supposed to do."

"No, I mean being there at the train station."

"Thank you for the invitation to that event, amigo," he said, grinning. "I like to see the branches of law enforcement in support of one another."

When he'd gone, I walked back to the cells and confronted the Thorndykes.

"What brought you boys back to Bear Creek on my wedding day?"

They looked at each other. "We came to kill *you*," Henry said.

"You're kidding, right?"

"Hell no, we ain't kidding, you son of a bitch!" Harvey swore.

"Why? Why would you risk everything just to get me?"

Henry scowled at me.

"You ruined everything the first time you ever showed up in Thorndyke, interfering in our business. You got our father killed and our ranch stole from us. You got to pay for that. We figured robbing the bank right under your nose would be a pretty good start. It would gall you when you found out it was us what done it."

Bob Logan had warned me they might try something like this.

"It was a stupid move. You led me right to your banker and your ranch."

"Yeah, we heard you caught our banker and Russel over there," he said, jerking his head toward the cell their partner, Tom Russel, occupied. "We got nothing left to lose now."

"Y'all did it to yourselves. Your father brought about his own destruction. I only got involved in any of this because y'all tried to ride rough shod over anyone who got in your way. Y'all lost the ranch when you became outlaws. That was your choice; I had nothing to do with it."

"Our pa built Thorndyke and the Diamond T from nothing, and we wasn't about to let no squatters and rustlers take any of it away from us, piece by piece."

I shook my head.

Turning to leave, I said, "What a waste."

"It ain't over yet," Henry said.

"It is for you," I said, walking away.

Dan Arnold

19.

"Dearly beloved, we are gathered together in the sight of God, to join together these two people; John Everett Sage and Lora Elizabeth O'Malley, in the bonds of Holy Matrimony," Brother Wes Spradlin began the ceremony.

My mind drifted a little.

How strange it was to be standing there, wearing a fancy suit the Governor of Colorado had given me himself. I was standing there unarmed while a notorious gunman performed our wedding ceremony.

I remembered my first wedding to Katya and how it had gone badly. I remembered the birth of our son, Nicolae, and how Katya had taken him and disappeared from my life for nearly two decades, only to be found again right here in Bear Creek. I thought about how uncertain and often surprising life is.

I looked at Lora. She was stunning and radiant. Her wedding dress was the color of champagne, with fancy lace trim and several little pearls sewed onto it. Her hair was beautiful, and there were pearls in the veil as well. The pearls had been my wedding gift to her, brought back from California. Becky had done an amazing job of keeping my secret until Lora went to put on the finished dress and veil.

As I looked at her, everything else, all the worries and memories went away.

***

Eventually, Wes Spradlin said, "You may kiss the bride," and I sure did!

When I turned and saw how many people crowded the church, all seats filled, and people standing in the side aisles and all the way out the back doors, I was stunned. Did these people really care that much about Lora and me?

I figured probably not, but everybody loves a good show.

It was time to head outside, to the reception.

As we started down the center aisle everybody cheered and clapped. Consuela was there with her family. Jacob and Sarah were with her.

I winked at them as we went by, and Lora gave them a big smile. I wondered what they thought of all this celebration and how different today was for them, compared to the day before.

Outside, a huge tent was set up over long rows of tables and chairs. There were other tents for cooking, and one tent was a makeshift saloon, with a bar made of boards and beer barrels. The food and drink had all been provided by the Palace and the Bon Ton.

I couldn't wait to see the bill.

There was even a simple dance floor built of boards with the band all gathered at one end. Tom and Becky led us to a table at one end of the giant tent where the wedding party and the gunslinger/preacher were to be seated.

Tom was fairly bubbling with enthusiasm.

"Now then, you two just stand here, and say howdy to the folks for a while. Whooee! I'll bet there are at least two hundred people here, and it ain't even time to eat yet. Wait till the band gets warmed up and the beer starts to flow! Uh oh! Here comes that newspaper man with his camera. I'll head him off, John."

"No wait, Tom, it's all right. I'd like to get a picture made of Lora and me. You and Becky should be in it as well."

***

Within a few minutes we stood posed the way the photographer wanted us. He took a picture of Lora and me, then he took another with Tom, Becky, Lora and I, standing together.

When I saw the picture in the newspaper the next day, I was pleased and a little surprised at how snazzy we all looked.

While we were standing there, posed for the camera man, I spotteed Bob Logan near the front of the crowd getting ready to come and greet us. He was all polished up and looked nothing like a drifting cowboy, a bounty hunter, or a deputy sheriff, for that matter.

Today Bob was the epitome of the wealthy gentleman. That was the way Bob liked to live, high on the hog, till the money ran out. Then he would be back dogging somebody's trail or hired out as a gun hand in someone's personal war.

We grinned at each other as he approached.

"Lora, may I say you are the single most stunning bride I have ever seen. I am only disappointed in your choice of husband," he winked at me as he kissed her on the cheek.

"Hello, Bob, so nice of you to come to the wedding. We've missed you, but I'm not in the least disappointed," Lora replied dryly.

He and I shook hands. He looked me over, nodding his approval.

"Congratulations, Sheriff. I'm surprised you were able to get her to the altar. I thought you would surely slip up and expose your true nature by now."

"Yeah, well, good men are hard to find," I chuckled.

"Glad you admit it." He turned back to Lora. " He may be the groom, but clearly I am the best man," he said.

"Sure, Bob, you're a legend in your own mind," Lora replied.

That comment made him laugh. He bowed slightly and said, "Mrs. Sage, you have proven yourself to be a fine judge of character."

She beamed at him.

"Bob, you are the first person to call me Mrs. Sage, and I quite like the sound of it."

***

We were greeted by the mayor, and accepted the warm wishes of dozens of people until the band finally struck up and it was time to dance.

And then we danced.

I was surprised at how good the music was. The first time I'd heard music in Bear Creek, it was a dreadful marching band.

It seemed as if everyone in town had come to our wedding, and it was nearly true. I thought briefly we'd better not have a fire, because the whole fire brigade was at the reception, along with the mayor, the judge, most of the county commissioners, and nearly all the police and sheriff's deputies.

***

We'd arranged for Tom and Becky to take care of Jacob and Sarah, planning to meet up with them at church the next morning. Good thing, too. It'd been an eventful day.

By eight o'clock or so, I was plumb tuckered out. Well, that was as good an excuse to leave the reception as any.

Shorty brought the carriage around, and Lora and I piled in the back as the crowd cheered and whistled.

Shorty drove us home.

Dan Arnold

20.

The pounding on the door woke us up at about eleven thirty—on our wedding night.

I jerked awake, not sure where I was for a moment. Lora and I lay wrapped up in each other's arms, both naked. I leapt to my feet, unsure what to do. Lora looked over at me standing there in the moonlight and she started laughing! I guess I must have looked kind of ridiculous.

I lit a lamp, grabbed my pants, and pulled them on quick, wishing I'd brought my guns. The pounding on the door didn't stop till I was going down the stairs carrying the lamp.

When I opened the door, there stood Buckskin Charlie. He was still dressed in his Sunday finest, but with his hat in his hands and a mortified look on his face.

"Evening, Charlie, what's the emergency?"

"Ahhhh, John, I'm so sorry to bother you like this, but . . . well, we discussed it and figured we just had to tell you tonight."

"Tell me what? Get to the point."

"They're gone, John, been gone for hours."

"Who's gone?"

"Those Thorndyke boys; somebody broke them out of jail while we were all at the party."

My head was spinning. It'd been a pretty eventful day.

"How in the hell did that happen?" I roared.

"I know, John, I'm sorry. Ed and Felix were at the jail. Felix was guarding the prisoners, and Ed had gone to get some sleep. Apparently they forgot to bar the door and somebody—Ed thinks it was the youngest Thorndyke boy—anyway, he walked right in and got the drop on Felix."

"Is he okay?"

"Felix? He's got a bad knot on his head, but I think he'll be okay."

Lora came down the stairs wearing a heavy robe and holding another lamp.

"Good evening, Charlie. I was about to make a pot of coffee. Won't you come in?"

"Oh . . . uh . . . no, thank you, Miss Lora, I'm sure sorry to bother you like this."

"Nonsense, Charlie, please come in. John, don't make Charlie stand out there on the porch. You might want to finish getting dressed, before you take a chill."

Stepping aside I motioned for Charlie to come in. Lora was right, being as I was both barefoot and bare chested, I did feel the night air.

I closed the door.

"Ed, we'll need to get on their trail . . ."

He shook his head.

"I don't think so, John. They've been gone for hours, and we don't have a clue where they went. There are no tracks on the brick streets, so we don't even know what direction they took when they left the courthouse. It's Saturday night, so the saloons were doing pretty good business, and there were people out on the streets. We talked to a number of people, and nobody noticed anything out of the ordinary. I think they left on foot, one or two at a time, maybe headed in different directions. They took that Russel feller with them."

"Alright, give me a few minutes to get dressed."

As I got dressed, I thought about what Charlie had said.

He was right. There was no way we could pick up their trail in the middle of the night. Still, there were things I needed to know. I walked down to the kitchen and found Charlie eating a piece of Lora's peach pie.

"The coffee is almost ready, John," Lora said.

"Thanks, baby."

"John, I don't think there's much point in you coming out tonight. We've pretty much done as much as we can do," Charlie pointed out.

"I expect you're right, Charlie, but I need to talk to Felix and Ed. Why didn't Ed hear what was going on?"

"Ed was asleep in the dormitory down at the other end of the basement. His shift wasn't really supposed to start till midnight. Felix was knocked out cold and then bound and gagged. He woke up lying on one of the beds in a locked cell. That's where I found him. You can go over all this with those fellers tomorrow. We just figured you needed to know what happened, so's you wouldn't be ignorant if somebody asked you about it first thing in the morning."

"You got that right. Good thing you went into the jail to check on things, when the party was over."

"Well, that's my job, and that particular party ain't over yet."

Lora poured us both a cup of coffee.

"Really, you mean folks are still dancing and what not?" She asked.

"I expect so. When I got to the jail and realized what happened, I sent Ed back there to gather up some of the other deputies and tell Tom about it."

"The news will be all over town by now."

Charlie shook his head.

"I reckon not. Ed said the party was rip-roaring when he got there. He took Tom aside and told him, private like. Then he told one of the other deputies to quietly spread the word to meet back at the jail. That's what they done. I doubt there was much of a stir."

"How long ago did this happen?" I asked.

"I got back to the jail at about ten o'clock. They'd been gone for more than an hour by that time."

"How did you get here, Charlie?"

"I walked. It only takes about fifteen minutes to walk down here from the courthouse. On the way down, I could still hear the music playing over at the party."

"Charlie, I need you to stay here with Lora, while I go up to the courthouse."

"Sure boss, but why do you need to go to the courthouse?"

"Walk outside with me for a minute, will you?"

I glanced over toward Lora, who had her back to us, as she added wood to the cook fire in the stove.

Charlie met my eye, and nodded his understanding.

"I just need to talk to Felix and Ed. I don't want them worrying and waiting till tomorrow."

Out on the porch, I told him why the Thorndykes had come to Bear Creek. They'd come to kill me.

"I don't have my guns with me tonight, Charlie; I left them at the courthouse when I got dressed for the wedding. Lora has a shotgun in the wardrobe in our bedroom, but I don't know if it's loaded or if she could use it in a pinch. I need you to stay here and keep your eyes open, while I go get heeled."

"Damn boss, I sure hate for you to be walking back into town without a gun."

"Yeah, me too, but I should've planned better. Keep your eyes open, and take care of Lora."

***

I'd just reached the corner of the first block of houses when I sensed someone was near.

"Easy, John, it's just me," Bob said. "I've been watching the house and the street."

He stepped out of the shadows under the trees, into the moonlight where I could see him.

"I came straight over here when I heard what happened. I've been here nearly an hour, but other than our friend, Buckskin Charlie, the only traffic I've seen has been that which one would expect to see on a Saturday night.

"Thanks, Bob. I guess you figured they might try to get me at the house."

"The possibility crossed my mind."

"They would've caught me flat footed. My guns are at the courthouse; that's where I'm headed. Charlie is staying at the house with Lora."

Bob drew his gun and handed it to me, butt first. I took it and tucked it into my waistband.

"Thanks, I don't guess this will leave you unarmed. I expect you have another gun."

He nodded. "I have more than one, actually."

It dawned on me the place Bob had been standing in the shadows was the exact spot where I'd seen the cigarette smoker several days earlier.

"Bob, have you been watching the house on other nights?"

"Heavens no, old man! Why on earth would I do such a thing? As much as I enjoy seeing Lora, that sort of behavior would have to be considered most unchivalrous."

I stepped into the shadows and struck a match. There were several cigarette butts on the ground. Clearly someone had been standing here smoking, on more than one occasion. The weeds and grass were pretty well trampled down. It didn't prove anything but it made me uncomfortable.

"How long have you been in town, Bob?"

"I've been enjoying the lesser aspects of the city for nearly a week. Why do you ask?"

"What brought you to town? You didn't check in with me. I'm guessing there's a pretty good reason."

"Indeed. It seems you know me better than most people do."

"I expect there was a profit motive; you were staying undercover. Who were you tracking?"

He chuckled.

"I came back to Bear Creek hot on the trail of young Homer Thorndyke."

Dan Arnold

21.

If Bob had been in Bear Creek nearly a week after following Homer Thorndyke here, then it meant Homer had been here at least as long.

"I guess you'd better tell me the whole story."

"I will be happy to do so; where would you like me to begin?"

"I know you captured Howard Thorndyke in Chaparral County at Mrs. Poole's Boarding House and took him to Denver. After you collected the reward, how did you get on Homer's trail?"

"That is as good a place to begin as any, although it is actually just a singular point in a continual progression . . ."

"Bob," I growled.

"Right, sorry. My point is that I had picked up the trail in Thorndyke one day after they came into town to visit the bank. I learned the Thorndyke boys were fairly regular customers at Mrs. Poole's. Homer, in particular. It seems he is kind of sweet on one of the girls there."

"Yeah, I think I've met her." I knew immediately I shouldn't have mentioned it.

"Really, does Lora know?" he grinned.

"Bob, I stopped by there in my official capacity."

"Oh, I'm sure you did."

"Get back to your story."

In the moonlight, he managed to look both wounded and annoyed.

"As I was saying, Homer never missed an opportunity to visit with the young lady in question. I staked out the location and waited for him to show up. Imagine my surprise and concern when Howard showed up first."

"I know this part, Bob. Tell me what happened after you left Denver."

"Isn't it obvious? I went back to Mrs. Poole's, figuring to wait for Homer, only Homer was just leaving when I arrived. He was traveling in the company of two other men, and I didn't find an opportunity to attempt his apprehension. Three against one was a little more than I cared to attempt. One plays the odds, after all."

"So, to sum up, I guess you followed Homer and those other two men back here to Bear Creek. Is that it?"

"It is, yes. When I drifted into town behind them, I was initially unable to determine their exact location. For days I searched. I tried all of the hotels, but they were not in any of them. I spent quite some time looking for them, even that last night, but was unable to find them. Imagine my surprise when they pulled off the bank robbery the very next morning. I was in a fine bed without a care in the world and totally unprepared in the event."

"I'll bet you hadn't thought any of the Thorndykes would show up in Bear Creek, much less all of them."

"Actually, John, if you will recall, I told you if you didn't go after them, they would be coming for you."

"It appears you were correct. This last robbery put me back on their trail and forced their hand."

"By the time I learned the details of the robbery, the posse was already heading out to meet you. At that point I had no idea the Thorndyke's were the culprits. I thought I was still on the trail of Homer, alone, and I thought he was still here in town. I had my suspicions of course, as one will, given the fact Homer and two other men had come into town and managed to disappear."

"It might've been helpful, Bob, if you'd bothered to inform me."

"Well, as I say, I spent quite some time looking for them, and . . ."

"And there was the profit motive."

"Indeed, I did have my eye on that reward money."

"I expect you still do."

"Well, I was terribly disappointed this morning when you paraded Henry and Harvey right through town. Their apprehension would have provided me with more than a year's wages as a deputy. Now, the circumstances have changed again and opportunity knocks, as they say."

I shook my head.

"It appears we have a conflict of interest."

"Not in the least, I want to see them stopped as badly as you do. By the way, the reward now offered has been changed to *dead or alive*."

I thought about all the implications of that.

"And, once the word of the jail break gets out, I expect the reward money will be increased yet again, possibly even doubled." He said, smiling.

I scowled at him.

"Oh, don't concern yourself with me, John. I have no intension of broadcasting the news of the escape. It will come out just as surely as the sun comes up in the morning."

I left him there, watching the house, and walked on into town. I couldn't hear any music playing over at the church grounds, so I figured the reception party was finally over. There was still some traffic on the square, and the lights were on at the Palace. I could hear some music over that way.

I nodded at a uniformed policeman standing on a corner near the square.

At the courthouse, I found the door bolted and had to knock to get it opened. *"Nothing like closing the barn door after the cow gets out,"* I thought.

Ed opened the door and on seeing me, he mumbled, "Oh gee, John, I'm sure sorry. If you want my badge . . . ."

I held up my hand. "Stop right there. Is this your fault?"

"Well, no; at least I don't think so."

"I don't think so either. Was this door locked when you went to bed?"

"See, that's the thing. I thought sure it was locked and barred, but Felix says the guy walked right in on him with his gun drawn and whacked him, without even saying a word. He never heard him coming."

I nodded. "Did you go upstairs and look to see if the doors are all locked up there?"

"No, I didn't even think of that. I've been too busy since the breakout."

"Go check it out. I want to talk to Felix."

"He's back there at the cells. We've still got two prisoners locked up."

The first thing I did was go into the dorm and strap on my gun belt, then I shrugged into my shoulder holster. Now, including the one that Bob had loaned me, I had three guns, and I didn't feel the least bit awkward. I walked down to the cell block, and found Felix sitting in the chair behind the desk with his back to a wall, facing toward the hallway. There was dried blood on the left side of his shirt and a soiled bandage around his head. He looked pretty miserable. There were a couple of the other deputies standing around.

"How are you feeling, Felix?"

He touched the side of his head gingerly.

"I'll live. I took a pretty good crack on the head though, makes me feel sick."

"Tell me what happened."

He closed his eyes for a moment.

"I was sitting right here, reading the newspaper. I heard or felt something moving, and I looked up just in time to see this guy swinging a pistol at my head. I never heard the door open or anybody coming down the hall. I didn't even have time to duck. He laid that pistol barrel up the side of my head. The next thing I knew, I woke up feeling like I was drowning. He'd cuffed my hands behind my back and stuffed a gag in my mouth. I guess he dragged me into a cell and locked the door, because that's where the Chief Deputy found me. I'm still pretty groggy."

I nodded. I could hear someone hurrying down the hall toward us. In a moment, Ed rounded the corner.

"I found most of the doors upstairs all locked, but the County Clerk's office door was standing wide open and a window of the Clerk's office was broken. It looks like that was the way he got into the building. He broke the window and crawled in. With the doors all closed and locked, nobody would have heard the window break, if he was careful. He unlocked the door of the clerk's office from the inside. He didn't make any sound coming down those marble stairs, and I guess he just slipped down the hall real quiet like and snuck up on you, Felix. I'm sure sorry."

"It's not your fault, Ed. We need to make some changes to the security around here. We'll need to put bars or something on all those windows upstairs. We'll need different locks on all the office doors as well. We can't have people breaking into any part of the courthouse," I said.

"I never even thought about it." Ed said

"This is on me, Ed. I'm the Sheriff. Well boys, it's well past midnight by now. Felix you need some rest. I'm going home. Ed, you've got the jail duty, right?"

"Yes sir."

"Okay then. Charlie will be coming back here in a little while. Don't let him sneak up on you." I immediately regretted saying it. I saw the crushed look on Felix's face.

"Felix, this was not your fault. None of y'all is responsible for this. The responsibility rests with me. You need to see the doctor. One of you men go with him."

I walked back to the dorm, gathered my satchel and saddle bags, and headed for home.

Dan Arnold

22.

The Sunday edition of the Bear Creek Banner had a more positive announcement by way of a headline:

BANK ROBBERS CAPTURED
SHOWDOWN AT THE STATION
The story went on to say:

"Police Chief Tom Smith and other law enforcement officers apprehended two of the fugitives involved in the daring daylight robbery of the first National Bank of Bear Creek, which occurred last week. The two men have been identified as Henry Thorndyke and Harvey Thorndyke, lately of Chaparral County. The two men surrendered to officers at the railroad station early yesterday afternoon.

Police Chief Smith is to be commended on the arrest, which proves that law enforcement does not need to involve violence.

A spokesman for the police department informs us the two men are being held in the Alta Vista County jail, awaiting arraignment on charges stemming from the robbery and other suspected crimes."

I found the wedding photo with Tom, Becky, Lora, and I, all standing together, on page three. The story said:

"County Sheriff John Sage and Mrs. Lora O'Malley were married in a service at the Bear Creek Community Church at four o'clock on Saturday afternoon."

"All the news that's fit to print," I mumbled.

I was relieved the story of the breakout had not yet hit the presses. I couldn't wait to see what that headline would be.

***

Even though we hadn't gotten much sleep on our wedding night, Lora and I were in the habit of going to church on Sunday. People were expecting us to be there. When we arrived at the church, we found Jacob and Sarah with Tom and Becky. I was startled to see Jacob and Sarah were dressed in Sunday-go-to-meeting clothes. It dawned on me they'd been similarly dressed at the wedding.

"Have you seen the newspaper?" Tom asked.

"Let it go, Tom," I replied. "I thought the wedding photograph was excellent."

"So did I," Lora added.

We were all in agreement on that point.

"My, don't y'all look good this morning. Sarah, that dress looks beautiful on you," I said, kneeling down in front of her and Jacob.

"Becky, however did you manage this?" Lora asked, running her fingers over the ribbon in Sarah's hair.

"Why there was nothing to it. It just so happens I'd already worked up Jacobs's clothes to sell at the general store. There aren't many readymade outfits for little boys in stock right now. Sometimes people don't want to wait for things to come from the catalogue company. I only needed to sew up the hem on the pants. Sarah's dress and whole outfit were hand me downs from Nora Adams. Tom bought Jacob's shoes at the general store yesterday. We'll have them both outfitted in no time."

"How do you like those shoes, Jacob," I asked.

"Not much!" he said, making a face. We all laughed.

People went out of their way to come and greet us. "Howdy to you, Mr. and Mrs. Sage," Bill Courtney said as he approached with his wife, Annabelle, and their daughter, Lacey.

"I didn't expect to see y'all here today. I know y'all stayed for the reception last night." I said.

"We stayed at the Front Range Hotel last night," Bill said. "Say, John, can I speak to you alone for a moment?"

I nodded.

"If you ladies will excuse us . . . ."

We walked away, over toward where the wagons and buggies were parked.

"John, I'll get straight to the point. How well do you know Bob Logan?"

"Pretty well, I guess. I've known him for several years. You know the Governor recommended him to you, and he saved my life last year. Why do you ask?"

"He worries me. Sure, I know the Governor recommended him, but he recommended him as a private detective. What he really is, is a hired gun fighter."

"What's the problem, Bill?"

He took a deep breath and considered for a moment.

"Well, it's Lacey. You know she and my foreman, Glen Corbett, are kind of sweet on each other?"

I nodded. Everybody knew that.

"Glen is a good man."

"Yes, John, he is a *very* good man. He's the kind of man who builds for the future, a man you can depend on, and that's the problem."

"I'm sorry, Bill, I don't understand."

"I'd like to see Glen and Lacey married and carrying on with the ranch. You know, after I'm gone."

"Sure. Makes sense to me. What's the problem?"

"Something's come between them.

"Well, that's sort of their business. I wouldn't want to mix in."

"But, Bob Logan *is* mixing in . . . ."

Now I understood why Bill was coming to me. Bob has an eye for the ladies, and Lacey is a beauty. Some time back, Bob had indicated to me he intended to try to get close to her. I discouraged him, pointing out that Glen and she were well on the way to being a married couple.

""Indeed, I observed that. However, there is no ring on her finger, and 'There's many a slip between cup and lip.'" I expect she is available, and she is not indifferent to my charm." He had grinned.

"Few women are, Bob, but it's not a good idea for you to interlope."

"*Au contraire, mon ami*. She is beautiful, single, available, and quite rich. I think it is a very good idea. He added, "Fortune favors the bold.""

At the time, I didn't like it, but it was none of my business.

Maybe it was my business now.

"Tell me what happened, Bill," I said.

"Last night, at the reception, Bob Logan basically hogged all of Lacey's attention. She danced more dances with him than anyone else, including Glen."

I winced. Bob tends to get what he wants.

"Glen spoke to her about it, and they had a spat."

"I'm sorry to hear that, Bill, but Lacey had a hand in all of it, and it isn't any of my business."

"It gets worse. When we got back to the hotel, they had a really bad falling out. Lacey said she thought she preferred Bob's company to that of Glen. Glen is ready to challenge Bob Logan to a fight."

"That would be a very bad idea, Bill. You're right, Bob is a killer. Glen wouldn't have a chance."

"I know, and that's why I sent Glen back to the ranch. Is there anything you can do to discourage Mr. Logan from courting Lacey?"

I thought about it for a moment.

"I'll speak to him, Bill, but is there anything you can do to dissuade Lacey?"

He frowned, looked away and then back at me, sighing.

"I hope so, but Lacey is both stubborn and headstrong. She's being fickle and unfaithful to Glen. She says Bob Logan is 'dashing.' Lacey tends to do as she pleases and get what she wants."

"If she gets Bob, she'll regret it for the rest of her life. In fact, we all will," I said. "And if Glen challenges Bob, he won't live five minutes. I think we should both speak to Glen about this."

Bill nodded.

"Thanks, John. I know it isn't your responsibility."

"It is if I can help prevent a killing."

***

Brother Spradlin's sermon that morning was on the value of not holding grudges or being easily offended.

"Remember, Jesus had all the power of the universe at His disposal, but he never raised His hand against those that slandered His name, spat in His face, beat Him bloody, and eventually crucified him on a cross. He humbled Himself in obedience to the will of the Father. Can you imagine how hard it must've been to be so ridiculed by your own creation, by the very people you came to save? Brothers and sisters, we are not superior to anyone, and we have no right to take offense at slights or petty offenses. Let them go. Forgive those who sin against you, . . ."

***

After the service ended, as we were heading outside, Wes Spradlin greeted us at the door.

"Sheriff Sage, could you wait a few minutes. I'd like to have a word with you."

I looked at Lora.

"Please don't be long, John. We need to feed these kids and Sarah is about ready for a nap," She said.

"Actually, that's what I want to speak to you about. Could I come by your home later?"

Lora gave him a big smile.

"Yes of course, Brother Spradlin. We would be delighted to have you. Won't you come for Sunday dinner? It'll just be fried chicken and corn on the cob, collard greens and mashed potatoes with gravy," Lora offered.

"Why, yes ma'am, I'd like that very much."

"Do you know where we live?"

"I surely do."

"Good, we'll look forward to seeing you, in about an hour."

Dan Arnold

23.

Sunday dinner with our new preacher proved to be enjoyable. Wes Spradlin showed us a side of himself I would never have imagined existed. He and I had played with Jacob out in the yard while Lora finished up the meal preparations and Sarah was napping.

We played baseball, using a ball and bat Wes brought with him. It wasn't the first baseball bat I had seen in Bear Creek. The Bear Creek Fire Brigade had formed a team, and some of my deputies had recently joined up with the police department to form a law enforcement team. I knew baseball was becoming quite popular all over the country. The Cincinnati Red Stockings had fielded an all professional team for at least twenty years. Chicago had been paying players for years. I'd heard the Boston Red Stockings now fielded a team of all professional, paid players. There'd been an organized national baseball league, started during the War Between the States, but this was the first time I'd ever actually touched a baseball.

I played the part of catcher and Wes pitched the ball. Jacob was the batter. At first, Jacob had a hard time even holding the bat. I suppose Wes and I improvised the rules a little, and, in no time, Jacob started hitting the ball.

***

After Lora's fine dinner, the kids were outside playing and we were sitting around the table in the dining room having coffee and conversation.

"May I ask what you plan to do with those two children?" Wes asked.

Lora and I looked at each other.

"Pastor Spradlin, at this point, there are too many things we don't know. Those poor kids are just now beginning to trust us enough to even speak. We don't know what happened to their parents. We don't know if they might have extended family somewhere. We don't know what to do." Lora said.

"We plan to provide for them as best we can until we find their family," I added.

"Oh, of course, I'm confident you will. The only reason I ask is because, as you know, there are several orphans on the streets here in Bear Creek, and our church is part of the group formed to address the issue. This is something altogether new for me. I don't have a clue where to start."

I considered that for a moment.

"Wes, It happens there's a local business woman who wants to donate some land and a two story house to the county, to be used as a school and orphanage."

Lora looked startled.

"Where did you hear that?" she asked.

"Mrs. Poole came to see me yesterday morning. She came specifically to make that proposal. We've been a little too busy to discuss it."

"Did you say Mrs. Poole, Mrs. *Emma* Poole?" Wes asked.

I nodded.

"Do you know her?"

"I used to. She knew me, way back when. I had no idea she was here in Bear Creek." Wes looked shaken.

Lora opened her eyes very wide and raised her eyebrows, making a face, as though she were saying, "Oh my!"

"I don't believe Mrs. Poole's Boarding House is even in Alta Vista County, is it, John?" Lora asked, rather casually.

"No, and she doesn't own that place. It belongs to the mayor of Waller. The property in question is up in North Fork."

"I had no idea she was here," Wes repeated.

"Well, it sure is a small world, isn't it?" Lora said, with a 'gee whiz' kind of grin.

"You must understand! I was a different person back then. I wasn't a good man at all." Wes said.

"After all these years, don't you think she's forgotten?"

"No, John, I expect not. I killed a man over her. She'll never forget it. I killed her husband."

***

How easy it is for passions to turn violent and end with killing. In the history of the world, how many men have been killed in fights over a woman? Human weakness and our sinful nature are always with us. All too common is that story.

Still, no matter how common it may be, an announcement like the one Wes just made does have a tendency to cause a pause in polite conversation.

We could hear the children playing outside.

After a moment, Lora said, "If you gentlemen will excuse me, I'll go check on the children."

We stood up as she left the room.

Wes shook it off, and breathed a deep sigh.

"It's funny how the past has a way of catching up to you," he said.

I nodded. If anyone understood that, it was me.

"How do we move forward from here," he asked.

"I have business up in North Fork. When I go up there the next time, you could ride along with me. We'll look over the property and see if it will actually be suitable for the intended purpose. If it is, the County will have a hard time explaining why they aren't interested in getting the orphanage started. It will cost them next to nothing. Of course, there is still the issue of staffing the place and budgeting for the ongoing maintenance, and so on."

"Not to mention rounding up the children," Wes added.

"We'll see how it all shakes out," I said.

"Do you think there will be a problem if I'm involved?" Wes asked.

"Is there still bad blood between you and Mrs. Poole?"

"I don't know. We haven't seen each other in several years. All that happened long ago and far away from here. At the time, she indicated she had little cause for sorrow at the loss of that particular gentleman. On his best days, he was a bad man and generally worse than worthless. He was a parasite who abused her."

"Okay, good, we'll plan on going to North Fork and checking out the property. Do you have a horse?"

"I have both a horse and a buggy. They actually belong to Bud and Mildred, but they are available for my use while I'm here."

"While you're here? Are you planning on going somewhere?"

"It depends to some degree on what happens with Bud's situation. They may or may not return, but if things go well, they may be able to return in a few weeks. I don't know. In any event, I may need to move on to a location a bit more off the beaten path."

"Why is that?"

"I am not the same man I was, but the rest of the world doesn't know it. I made enemies in my wilder days, and while I've learned to forgive those who've sinned against me, there are those who may come hunting me because they are not the forgiving type. Then there is the matter of my reputation. Bear Creek is a little too easy to find for anyone who might come hunting trouble."

I spent a moment considering the various implications of these things. Wes had a reputation as a gunman. He'd killed at least eleven men. Sooner or later, someone would come looking for him

"I understand. I expect it will take some time for you to redeem your reputation," I said.

"Yes, I can only hope I will live long enough to do it."

"I'll help in any way I can," I offered.

"Thank you, John. I intend to earn your trust."

"You know, I think we need to get started on this orphanage project as soon as possible. Do you want to go up to North Fork tomorrow, if I can get loose?"

"Yes, I would like that."

"Well, then, come by my office in the courthouse tomorrow morning. I have some serious issues to address and may not be able to get away. If it looks like I can get free, we'll head on up there."

24.

It seemed like Brother Spradlin had only just left, when Lora came back in with another visitor.

"Look what I found wandering around outside," she said.

Today, Bob was dressed in the manner of a working man. He wore a homespun red cotton shirt over wool pants, with a canvas jacket to cover his guns.

"Hey, Bob, what brings you by here this afternoon?"

Bob held his hat in his hands, looking casually around the room.

"Was that Wes Spradlin I saw leaving?"

"Yes, he's our new pastor. How do you know him?"

"A preacher? Not the last time I saw him. I don't actually know him, but I've seen him work."

"What are you referring to?"

"Can I take your hat, Bob? Won't you sit down?" Lora offered.

Bob surrendered his hat and bowed slightly.

"I guess it was five or six years ago, over in Arizona Territory. I was thinking about taking a job for a big rancher there in a serious conflict with another ranch over some water rights. Anyway, I had just gotten to the little town and was sitting in the only saloon—not to my standards, when Wes Spradlin came in. I had just met three men who worked for the same outfit I was thinking about hiring on with. Those three riders shaped up to be gun slicks rather than cattlemen. When Spradlin came in, they got real quiet and told me who he was and that Spradlin worked for the other outfit in the conflict.

Those three hombres had just enough whiskey in them to make them maybe a tad bit reckless. I don't know; maybe they figured three against one was pretty good odds, but for whatever reason, they braced Spradlin. They fanned out in front of him and started mouthing off with threats and telling him to quit the country. Your pastor there, Mr. Spradlin, had his back to the bar and he had nowhere to move.

I'll never forget it. He looked at those men and called them pansies and weak little sisters. He said real men would face him alone, or one at a time. He said those boys were lily livered cowards, and it was those words that opened the ball.

All three of them grabbed for their guns. The first one was pretty quick, but his shot missed Spradlin. When the shooting stopped, Spradlin was the only one standing. All three of those men were shot up and your 'holy Brother Spradlin' was calmly thumbing new shells into his guns, still casually leaning against the bar."

"He killed all three men? Lora asked, clearly shocked.

"Well no, I think one or more of them probably lived, but they were sure enough holey themselves, shot full of holes and finished with fighting."

"Oh my, that's horrible," Lora said.

"Indeed it was. Then, through the thick cloud of gun smoke, I saw Spradlin look over at me, to see if I wanted to try my luck. Now, I, being a man of sound mind and cleverer than most, decided right then and there I would seek other employment in a different part of the country."

"I just can't imagine Brother Spradlin could ever do something like that," Lora observed.

Bob shrugged and turned to me.

"I was hoping you and I could talk for a minute."

"Of course, but what's so urgent it can't wait till tomorrow?"

"It's about the matter we discussed at some length last night." He glanced toward Lora.

"Honey, would you bring Bob and me some coffee?"

Lora took the hint.

"This seems to be the day when I have to find busy work, so the men can talk," she huffed, as she turned and left the room.

"Alright Bob, what's up?"

"I've been all over town today, and I'm pretty sure our friends with a proclivity to rob banks have pulled out. I'm not certain they left, but I know that early this morning, someone bought three horses from the Mexican horse trader over by the fair grounds."

"It seems like kind of slim evidence. Is it your theory they headed east?"

"There's more. I learned four white men were sort of camped out in a place over on the other side of the tracks. One of those men was the one who bought the three horses this morning. He was a young fellow, perhaps twenty years of age. He rode in late last week, rented a house, and he was keeping his horse with the Mexican fella."

"Where were these men staying?"

"There is an old woman over there that was willing to rent out her house for a few days while she went and stayed with her daughter and son in law—the very same horse trader to whom I previously referred. She was upset because her house is small, and she rented it to one man, but when she went by her house early this morning on the way to mass, there were four men in there. She said one night last week there had been five men in the house."

"Hmmmmm, now that is a coincidence. How did you find out about all of this?"

"I told you, I spent the better part of a week trying to find young Homer Thorndyke. Money talks, and so did the old woman. She didn't like those gringos at all. She described them to me, and the description fits our missing bandits."

"Sounds about right. It explains why you couldn't find your man. Did they get horses from the son-in law?

"They did indeed."

"So they may have pulled out. They're gone and so are the horses?"

"Gone, but not forgotten."

"Well, that's sort of good news. It's a relief in a way. I'm glad they're no longer here in Bear Creek."

"They won't go far, John. They still want you dead."

We hadn't heard Lora's approach. "Who wants John dead?" she asked as she brought in a tray with coffee service on it.

Bob never missed a beat.

"Oh, you know, the usual assortment of crooked politicians, social climbers, riff raff, and jilted former lovers," Bob said.

Lora turned on me, "Tell me the truth, John. Why is everybody avoiding talking to you in front of me? Are you in danger?"

"It just goes with the job, Baby. I didn't want you to be upset by hearing about ugly aspects of the job."

"What is it? What's happened? Is it those Thorndyke brothers, the men who robbed the bank?"

"Yes. They've made some threats, but there's no need to worry. Bob was just telling me they've left town, and are now headed for parts unknown."

"Then you have to find them before they find you," she said, crossing her arms and setting her jaw.

I looked at Bob, and he smugly raised his eyebrows.

"Why Lora, I think you are correct. Those men do pose a threat to John. We should pursue them. I believe they are desperate and dangerous men given to acts of violence. What do you think, John?" Bob asked, feigning innocent interest.

"Well, I think, at this point, we don't have any idea where they may have gone."

"Actually, that may not be quite the case," Bob said.

"It doesn't really matter. They have nearly a full day's head start on us. It would take us some time to get organized and put together a posse. There's no way we could pick up a trail tonight, even if we knew which way they went, and that's assuming they all stayed together." I said.

"Permit me to address some of those comments in the order in which you have presented them. First, it does indeed matter. If we can determine where they may have headed, we can go there and confront them. Second, there is no need to go about trying to organize a whole posse this afternoon. Third, we don't need to try to track them at all. And, fourth, I believe they will all stay together."

"What gives you that idea, Bob?"

"Which idea? They are all quite good ideas, and the rationale is above reproach."

"Stop it,! Just tell me why you think you know where they may have gone."

"Well, John, I am a trained detective. I have become quite skilled at finding men who do not wish to be found. I have a keen intellect and the ability to arrive at reasonable conclusions based on deductive reasoning and assessment of the evidence at hand."

"Yeah, Bob, you're smarter than the average criminal. I'll give you that. And you have both experience and skill at tracking down fugitives. But dammit, so do I!"

"Of course, you do. If you would but stop and think for a moment, I believe you would be able to work through the available information, examine the various possibilities, define the probabilities, and make a decision about a course of action. Really, you are so distracted these days."

I considered beating the snot out of him right then and there, but I didn't want to hurt my hands—and it *was* Sunday.

I guess Bob, using his great powers of observation, was able to deduce that I was pretty annoyed.

"Let me ask you this; if you were a desperado and you knew you couldn't outrun the telegraph, and that every lawman within a hundred miles, to the north, south, or east was on the lookout for you; if you knew the local law would expect you to run to the east; if you knew you had to go somewhere where there was no real law, and where four rough men wouldn't be noticed or be in the least out of place—if those things were true, but you still needed to be close enough to Bear Creek so you would be able to sneak back into town on any given night, where would you go?"

I was pretty sure I knew where he was trying to lead me, but I needed to challenge his thinking.

"I might head west, up into the mountains, but that would be better for just one man alone. A party of four would leave a clear trail and run through their supplies pretty quickly, especially if they couldn't take much with them like that bunch had to do."

Bob made a "move along" motion with his hand, indicating he had already considered those things.

"The best thing to do would be to split up and take off in four different directions, every man for himself."

Bob grinned.

"Yes, that is what smart people might do under the circumstances. It brings into focus my reasoning as to why they won't split up."

"Which is?"

"First, three of them are brothers and have pretty much always hung together, to coin a phrase.

Second, any time in the past when they have split up, they have ended up being picked off, or arrested. There is safety in numbers.

Third, they are not smart. They are foolishly determined to accomplish one task, and can't grasp the fact they are just about done for.

Fourth, and this goes back to number three; they have an agenda. They want to kill you, and while it proves they are stupid; nonetheless, they are just smart enough to have learned that killing you is not a job to be tried alone."

He was right on each count. Still, I had one more thing to consider.

"They might force their way into someone's home or farm and hide out there."

"That would be very dangerous and might well attract attention. Don't forget; they know what happens to somebody trapped in a house when they are surrounded by armed men. They need to go somewhere where they won't raise any alarm."

I shrugged, conceding the point.

"Now then, considering all of that, and remembering their greatest weakness."

"And what do you believe that weakness is, beyond them just being stupid."

"They like whores, John. Pardon me, Mrs. Sage, for being indelicate, but John has missed his nap and has become quite impatient."

Lora scowled at him.

"So, to sum up; they will most likely stick together. They will flee into the mountains to the west, where there are no telegraph lines and there is no real law. They need to go somewhere where criminals are welcome, and the law is not, somewhere with food and shelter. They will want to be somewhere pretty close to Bear Creek. And, last but not least, somewhere where they can find female companionship. When you consider all of those probabilities, what town comes to mind?"

"North Fork," all three of us said, at the same time.

***

I walked out with Bob to where he'd tied his horse at the hitching rail by the front gate.

"I have to ask you why you came and told me this when you could go try to collect that reward money all by yourself?"

"I'm good, John, very good, but I'm not stupid. I can't take on all four of those men alone."

"You've been pretty good at finding the stray that wanders off from the herd."

"Yes, I have, and I know how to cut one out from the herd now and then, but this is different now."

"How so?"

"I don't think there is enough time. They will come for you as soon as they can drink up sufficient courage. They have nothing left to lose and nowhere to run. They are more or less literally backed into a corner."

" So will you come with me to go after them?" I asked

"Of course, I will go with you; I wouldn't let you go alone."

"In what capacity?"

"Pardon me, I don't follow." Bob said.

"Will you be coming with me in your capacity as my deputy, or as a bounty hunter?"

"Isn't it enough that I come with you?"

I nodded.

"It is, yes."

"Then we'll just have to wait and see how things work out, at the time."

"No, you're a deputy sheriff of Alta Vista County. We'll be going to recapture and arrest them. You can't claim any reward if you are acting as my deputy."

"John, there is a lot we don't know at this point, and there is a lot that can go wrong in this deal. We don't know for sure when, where, or how we will find them, not to mention how things will go once we actually do find them. I say let's just adopt a wait and see attitude."

"No," Lora called from the porch. I didn't know she was there and I wouldn't have thought she could hear us from there.

"There can be no waiting and there is only one way it can work out. You have to go find them, and do it quickly. You go find them and if you have to, you kill them; kill them all, before they can kill my husband."

"Yes ma'am," Bob called over to her.

He looked at me after he had stepped up on his horse.

"I'll tell you this; we would do well to take your wife's advice, it's time to put an end to them."

He swung away, trotting his big black horse up the hill into town.

Dan Arnold

25.

When I walked back up on the porch, Lora apologized.

"I'm sorry, John. I don't mean to butt into your business, but this involves me too. I won't have some two-bit killers hunting for you. Please find a way to put an end to this. This is not the way I want to start our marriage . . . or for our marriage to end."

I wrapped my arms around her, finding her a bit more stiff than usual.

"Yes ma'am. I understand how you feel. I never intended for any of this to happen."

She put her head against my shoulder.

"I know you didn't."

I kissed her. "Let's go check on those kids."

When we got to the backyard, we found them laughing and chasing each other around in circles. Jacob had taken off his shoes and socks. Sarah was still dressed in her Sunday frock and tights.

"We'll need to get them some play clothes," Lora observed.

"Yeah, but it looks like we can just skip buying any more shoes," I chuckled.

"Who wants milk and cookies?" Lora called.

***

Back in the house, we were sitting on the couch in the parlor. Jacob was sitting between us on the couch playing with a carved wooden horse. We didn't really have anything in the way of toys. Lora was sort of humming to Sarah where she lay curled in her lap.

I figured this might be a good time to ask a few questions.

"Jacob, how did you come to be living in Al's livery stable?"

He just shrugged.

"I mean, did you walk there or did someone give you a ride?"

"We walked," he said.

Lora looked at me over the top of his head and nodded. This was a positive sign. "Did it take a long time to walk there?"

He shrugged again.

"Where did you walk from?"

"We walked from the farm, after . . . ."

I waited for a moment.

"Where is the farm, Jacob?"

"It's down by Yellow Butte."

I knew where Yellow Butte was. It was about fifteen miles south and a little west of Bear Creek. I'd heard there were a couple of big ranches down in that country, and maybe a few farms scattered along Buttercup Creek. There was a rough road through the area. Yellow Butte was the name of the huge mesa at the edge of the mountains, and the name of the only town in the area was Buttercup.

"Do you know where Buttercup Creek is?" I asked.

He nodded. "Uh huh," he said.

"Is the farm near the creek?"

"Uh huh," he said again.

"Have you ever been up on Yellow Butte?"

"Yes, sir."

"Is the farm near the mesa?"

He shrugged. "It's right there. I mean we went up there all the time. It's right behind the house."

I didn't want to push, but I wanted to know why they had walked all the way to Bear Creek.

"Are there many animals on the farm?"

He shook his head.

"Not no more. We turned the milk cow loose when we left."

I decided to ask the question.

"Why did you leave?"

He was silent for a moment and stopped playing with the carved horse.

"There wasn't no food, and I was scared for Sarah."

I looked at Lora.

"Jacob, honey is your mother still on the farm?" she asked gently.

He nodded.

"Yes, Ma'am, only she's dead."

"Oh Jacob, I'm so sorry to hear that. Is your daddy still there?" she asked.

He shook his head.

"No, they kilt him somewheres else."

Lora had tears in her eyes. I had more questions of course, but I needed a break.

"Let's go see if the horses will come up for some carrots. Do you want to, Jacob?"

He shrugged again, but I could tell he was eager to go with me. The horses were always happy to come to the fence for handouts.

***

After the kids were in bed, Lora and I lay wrapped in each other's arms.

"Wes Spradlin and I are going up to North Fork tomorrow. I expect we'll leave a little late in the day, and we'll be up there the whole night. Will you be okay here by yourself?" I asked.

"I won't be alone. Consuela is coming in the morning. I think I'll take the kids into town and do some shopping. In the afternoon, I have some people coming by to see about maybe rooming here."

I'd forgotten about that.

"I'll hitch up the team first thing in the morning and drive y'all into town. That will work out well, as I can drive y'all back here on our way to North Fork."

"How convenient," she said dryly.

I let it go by.

"When I get back, I plan to ride on down to Buttercup. I want to try and find out what exactly happened to their parents."

I knew she understood I was thinking about Jacob and Sarah.

"Maybe they had other family in the area or a neighbor might know of someone. We could all go down there together. The kids could probably help us find the farm. We could have a picnic. They might want to go back and visit if nothing else," Lora suggested.

"A picnic is a good idea, but no, I don't think taking the kids down to Yellow Butte is a good idea, at least not at this point. I'm concerned about what happened to their parents. I don't want to put those kids through any more traumas or put you in danger. I can travel faster and cover more ground alone. Besides, I have a general idea where to look."

"That was disturbing, what Jacob said, wasn't it?" Lora asked.

I took a deep breath and let it out slowly.

"It sounds like there might be trouble in that part of the county. I'd like to ask Jacob some more questions, but . . . ."

"You were really good with him today. So gentle and yet you were able to get answers without being too firm."

"Thanks, but I'm sure no great shakes at it, especially not compared to you. I wish I knew more about them and could be more help to them."

"Just give it some time, John."

Dan Arnold

26.

"No, John! I don't like it. I think you would be better off taking most of the deputies and a dozen or so men in a posse," Buckskin Charlie said.

He, Bob and I were talking it over in my office, first thing, the next morning.

"I understand how you feel, Charlie, but I've done this sort of thing before. I'm telling you it's better to go with a small group that moves fast without drawing a lot of attention. Besides, we don't really even know if they went to North Fork."

"John, there is safety in numbers," Charlie insisted.

"So I've heard, but sometimes safety isn't the first consideration."

"Well, it should be!"

"Charlie, if we start pulling together a posse, somebody might very well send word up there ahead of us. We could ride into an ambush, or they could skedaddle before we got there. Nothing good could come from either of those events."

"Oh, for crying out loud, John! Maybe this and maybe that! A posse would give you enough men and guns to deal with either of those problems."

"I told Tommy Turner I had no plans to show up in North Fork with a posse. If I do, it will look like I went back on my word. I gave him thirty days to turn things around up there and I mean to give him the whole thirty days, Now, he won't mind me showing up with a couple of men to haul in some bad outlaws, but a posse would stir up a hornet's nest."

"Well, I don't like it."

"I heard you the first time. I can take Ed or another deputy instead."

"Like hell you will. I'm going, and that's all there is to it, but I still don't have to like it."

"I don't like anything about it," I said. "How about you Bob? You're being remarkably quiet this morning."

"I'm merely waiting for you two old ladies to finish squabbling so we can put together a timetable and a workable plan."

Charlie shot him a hard look.

"Okay. I was already planning to take the Pastor of our church, Brother Spradlin, up there today to look over a piece of property. That will be our reason for going into town. We'll plan to get there late in the day. The rest of us go in tonight, just after dark. We split up and come into North Fork from different directions. We act like we're just headed for the saloons, same as any other arriving riders. It will be dark, so there's little chance anyone will recognize any of us. Tommy knows me, but nobody else in North Fork really does. Of course, the bad news is the Thorndykes know all of us on sight. We'll have to be very careful."

Bob smiled grimly.

"What are you smiling about?" I asked.

"Actually, they don't know me to look at, as I have never drawn their attention. I have developed some skill at not being noticed. They only know you, Charlie, and the other deputies by sight.

Gentlemen, this is a good start. Now let's address how we search the town. What if they are not all together in exactly the same spot? For instance, even if they are all in the same saloon, they might not all be in the same room or sitting at the same table.

You start walking into well-lit buildings and someone up there will recognize you, and it won't take long to figure out you are searching for someone. The Thorndykes might just spot you the second you walk in the door and cut you down before you even know they're in there."

He was right. I had to hand it to him; Bob was good at this.

"What do you suggest?"

"I like the idea of just a few men going up there, and I agree we need to do it quickly. I'm the only one in this office who is unknown to them. They will be on the lookout for any possible threat. My suggestion is we agree on a time and place to meet up, right after dark.

While the sheriff and the Reverend Spradlin are doing whatever it is they need to do up there, I'll make the rounds through town and see if I can locate our quarry. I won't attract any unwanted attention. I'll meet up with the rest of you when and where we agree to meet. If they are in North Fork and I do locate them, then we can determine how we want to take them."

I looked at Charlie. He shrugged in response.

"Yeah, that just might work," I said. "We might be able to make it work even more efficiently if we add another man to help you do the searching. A man they don't know."

"Who do you have in mind?"

"Wes Spradlin," I said.

"The preacher?" Charlie asked. "How would he know what the Thorndykes look like?"

Bob grinned. "Oh I must say, I do like the way you think. Are you of the opinion he would serve in that capacity?"

It was my turn to shrug.

"It can't hurt to ask. How much more unthreatening can you be than a humble preacher just checking out the town?"

"The notion is sound, but there's nothing the least bit humble about him. He has spent a lifetime building the reputation as that of a deadly pistolero. As you know, I can personally attest to his expertise in that line of work. There is a wild and unsavory crowd up there in North Fork. Chances are somebody up there could know him from the old days."

I knew Bob was not the kind of person who could imagine it was possible for a man to change. I knew men didn't change without a real good reason, and I also knew Wes Spradlin really was a different man now. But there was no point in trying to explain any of it to Bob.

"Maybe, but don't you think it would make him seem even less likely to be involved with law enforcement?"

"Now wait a minute," Charlie said. "Are you saying your Preacher is the same man as Wes Spradlin the gunman?"

"Yes, Charlie, they are one and the same man."

"Jumpin Jehoshaphat!" Charlie spluttered.

There was a knock on the office door. "I expect that's him now. Come on in," I called.

"Sorry to bother you, Sheriff," Shorty said as he stuck his head in the door. He made a face. "The newspaper man from the Banner is here, and he insists on seeing you immediately."

You could have heard a pin drop in the room. We'd all seen the morning paper and had been relieved there was still no story about the jail break. The "big news" of the day was the amount of traffic through town, and especially around the square, was becoming nearly unmanageable. The collection and disposal of the manure created by so much horse traffic on the brick streets was barely adequate. Some days, the smoke from burning manure piles hung over the town.

With the appearance of the newspaper man, we could all see the likelihood there was about to be another and different kind of stinking mess.

I took a deep breath.

"Okay, Shorty, thanks. Ask him to wait a moment."

I looked around at the other men. Worry was clearly evident. They had the same thought I did. The news was about to spin out of our control.

"Okay, y'all let me deal with this newspaper man, and then we'll talk some more. I guess this meeting is adjourned."

27.

Jerry Starnes was the publisher, type setter, editor and principle reporter of the *Bear Creek Banner*. I say principle reporter because it seemed like half the women in town carried stories to him. In the paper, he always referred to himself as "this reporter." As in, *"This reporter has learned Wallace Watkins plans to sell the barbershop at his earliest convenience. Mr. Watkins is evidently contemplating a move to Denver where he plans to open a new barbershop."*

I guess he has to work hard to fill up the pages with something besides advertising.

"Mr. Starnes, I have another appointment this morning, so I can only give you a few minutes of my time."

He got right to the point.

"Tell me, Sheriff Sage, is it true the men who robbed the bank have escaped?"

"Where did you hear that?"

"Where I heard it is irrelevant; I have my sources. Is it true or not?"

"No comment."

"Oh no, Sheriff, not this time. I know for a fact those men have escaped. I don't believe you want me to write that you refused to comment on the facts."

I considered my response.

My policy had always been not to comment about anything to the press. It had worked well for me, but this time I wanted to try to do a little damage control.

He seemed to sense that.

"Mr. Starnes, I will make a statement, if and only if, you will consider my concerns and handle this matter in a way that will be impartial and not become a cause for public concern."

He glared at me.

"I'll tell you what I won't do. I won't do a whitewash job for you, or help you try to make this department look any less incompetent."

I gave him a cold stare.

"Alright, I'll hear what you have to say, but I'll print whatever I see fit."

I chuckled and shook my head. This guy was hopeless.

"I know you will."

"Well then, Sheriff, go ahead and say your say and try to make your case."

I could see there was no point in trying to explain my concerns to him, so I gave him my statement.

"Early Saturday night, a person whose identity is unknown at this time, broke into the County Clerk's office in the courthouse, crept downstairs and ambushed one of the deputies on duty. That deputy is now on leave recovering from injuries he received in the incident. The unknown man then assisted three prisoners in escaping. Two other prisoners remain incarcerated at this time, awaiting trial. The three men who escaped were suspects in an ongoing criminal investigation, but have not, as yet, been arraigned on the charges which prompted their arrest."

Starnes was furiously scribbling in his notebook. He looked up at me.

"Sheriff Sage, where were you while all this was going on?"

"It was my wedding night."

That shut him up for a moment.

"Why didn't you have more deputies guarding the prisoners?"

"I gave you my statement."

"Do you have any idea where the escaped prisoners may have gone?"

"You have my statement."

"Are they armed?"

"I've said all I'm going to say."

"Are they somewhere here in town?"

I stood up and walked over to my office door, opening it. I decided to add one thing to my previous statement.

"We have reason to believe the escaped prisoners have left the immediate area and that they pose no threat to the citizens of Bear Creek." I indicated the open door. "Thank you for you cooperation, Mr. Starnes. As I said, I have another appointment."

"Wait a minute. You said you had some concerns. What are your concerns?"

I paused for a moment. "I'm concerned about you." I looked him in the eye. "I'm concerned you will write a deliberately inflammatory story sensationalizing the escape and frightening the community. I would consider such action unwise, irresponsible, and an affront to this department."

"Is that all?"

I nodded.

"If I were you, I'd think about that *last* statement. Goodbye, Mr. Starnes."

"Huh!" He said, as he walked out of my office.

I stuck my head out into the hallway and saw Wes Spradlin talking to an older couple who were seated on a bench outside the Tax Office. When he saw me he excused himself and came over to my office. I brought him in and pointed to the chair most recently vacated by publisher Starnes.

"Busy day at the courthouse," he commented, sitting down with his broad brimmed black hat in his lap. "I'll understand if you can't get away to go up to North Fork today."

"Actually, I plan to do exactly that."

I paused to gather my thoughts. I suppose some strain was evident on my face.

"Is something bothering you, John?"

I chuckled.

"I guess you could say I have a love/hate relationship with the press. I love to hate the newspapers."

He nodded. I figured his relationship with the press had not been particularly positive either.

"And, there's something else ..."

He just looked at me, waiting and expectant. I decided to tell him the whole thing.

"We had a jail break on Saturday night after the wedding. Three prisoners escaped with the help of a fourth man. It was the holdup men that killed Ted Johansen during the bank robbery last week. One of my deputies got clubbed in the head by the fourth man and he's pretty sick; concussion I expect."

He nodded and continued to wait for me to go on.

"We think the fugitives may have gone up to North Fork."

He raised his eyebrows.

"I just wanted you to know this won't exactly be a pleasure trip. Two of my deputies will be going with us, and I plan to apprehend those men, if we find them there."

He nodded again.

"Okay, fine with me," he said.

He studied me for a moment.

"I take it there's more to the story?"

I sighed, as I thought about what to say next.

"You should know these men are particularly dangerous. They intend to kill me on sight. Now, I know you've become a man of the cloth, and I don't want to put you in danger…"

He held up a hand to stop me.

"John, I can take care of myself. I'm more concerned about you. I'll help in any way I can, but you need to focus on what has to be done. Would it be better if I stay here until after you do this?"

I shook my head.

"No, this trip up there with you gives me a pretense to be in North Fork. If anyone sees me and recognizes me they'll see that I'm with a preacher and might not think about me looking for anyone in particular. I'm going to try and avoid being recognized, but I can't make any promises."

"So, basically speaking, you want to use me as a disguise.

"Simply stated."

"Ok, I'm ready whenever you are."

"Well, there is one more thing."

He chuckled.

"Yeah, there usually is."

"When we get up there, I'm going to have to lay low and avoid the people on the streets and in the saloons and gambling halls, until we know exactly where those men are. Would you be willing to help look for them, the outlaws I mean? They don't know you, so they wouldn't be tipped off if they saw you. One of my deputies, Bob Logan, will be looking for them and they don't know him either."

Wes looked at me with kind of a wry smile.

"What is it?" I asked.

"It's just interesting to think of Bob Logan as one of your deputies."

"You know him?"

"Only the same way he knows me—just by reputation. You know how it happens. I've seen it happen to you right here in Bear Creek. People talk about a person who has done violence on one or more occasions, what they've done and what they're rumored to have done.

Newspapers need sensational stories to sell more newspapers and attract more advertisers, so they love shootings and killings. Pretty soon a man's name gets known and stories get exaggerated.

I've heard that Bob Logan is a bounty hunter and, occasionally, a killer for hire—the kind of man I used to be. Different from me though. His reputation is that of a man unseen, like a snake under a cupboard, or a scorpion in your boot, ready to strike at any moment. He's also been known to change his appearance and hide practically in plain sight.

I heard all those things about him, but then I met him at your wedding. Now that I've met the man, he is considerably more civilized and intelligent than I would have expected from his reputation alone. I expect he would make an excellent deputy. I understand he has a background as a detective."

I considered my answer.

"He worked as a Pinkerton agent before I hired him as a detective. I'll let you decide for yourself. I'll tell you this though—he's a little bit of everything you've heard about him and one thing more."

"What is that?"

"He's my friend."

Wes smiled.

"I hope you will consider me a friend."

"Thank you. I expect it's an imposition to ask for help in searching for escaped outlaws."

"Not at all, but I'll need a pretty detailed description of the men we'll be looking for."

"We'll go over all the details and do some further planning on our way up to North Fork. Can you meet us at my house at about one o'clock?"

28.

I was on my out, when Charlie rushed into my office.

"I'm sorry, John. I forgot all about it. I have to testify at those danged court hearings this afternoon. You know those two fellas, the assault, and the livestock theft. It plumb slipped my mind when you told me about those Thorndyke boys maybe being up in North Fork. You could take Ed or Shorty or somebody to go in my place, but I'm gonna need at least one deputy to help escort the prisoners."

"Don't worry about it, Charlie. We have to take care of business and that includes court appearances. With Felix out and Bob and me gone, it leaves just you, Ed and Shorty to handle the jail and escort the prisoners to and from the courtroom."

"Yeah, but you can't go up to North Fork with just one deputy. You'd better form a posse."

"We don't even know for sure they're in North Fork, and I already told you why I'm not taking a posse up there. No, Charlie, the situation hasn't changed. The plan stays the same."

"John, you don't have enough man power to round up four armed men. Maybe you could take Tom or someone from the police department."

"Tom is also tied up in court this morning, and this isn't his responsibility. Besides, I think we can handle this on our own."

"You mean you want to handle it on your own. I don't blame you for that, John, but it's too dangerous. Think of Lora . . . and them kids."

I gave Charlie a sharp look.

"Sorry, John. Okay, you're the Sheriff, and it's your decision. But I expect it's a good thing you're taking a preacher with you."

***

Although it was a beautiful sunny day in Bear Creek there was thunder rumbling in the far blue mountains, when I ran into Tom on the street.

"Good morning, Chief Smith. If you're done in court this morning, perhaps I could request the assistance of the police department in locating some missing persons."

"Well howdy, John. The police department stands ready to assist the sheriff's department in any way we can. Who has gone missing?"

"I can't seem to find my wife or the two children who are accompanying her this morning."

He chuckled.

"Problem solved and persons located! They're with my wife over at the railroad depot."

"Huh! What are they doing over there? I wouldn't have thought to look at the depot."

"Lora thought the children would enjoy watching the 12:10 to Denver come in to the station. Becky went along for the fun of it."

"We're supposed to be heading for the house about now," I grumbled.

"Yeah, it is pretty much lunchtime. Court's adjourned till one thirty. I'll go down to the station with you. I need to round up my wife as well."

I was feeling pressed for time. Bob and Wes were supposed to meet me at the house at one o'clock. I was hoping to enjoy whatever Consuela had cooked up, with just my little family, before Bob and Wes got there.

***

As we walked down to the station I told Tom what we were planning to do.

"I'll go with you up to North Fork if you like. It seems to me you might need a couple more men than you have."

I like Tom, and he's as good a policeman as he had been a good deputy, but two of the Thorndykes knew him by sight. If I got him killed, neither Becky nor my wife would ever forgive me. I wouldn't be able to forgive myself either.

"You were mighty handy the first time we caught them. I appreciate the offer Chief, but it's a little out of your jurisdiction, and I think we can handle it."

He shrugged.

"If anyone could handle it, it would be you and Bob. Still, having more men might prevent bloodshed."

I thought about it. I'd had four deputies and Tom with me when I arrested them the last time. Was I looking to start a fight? No, I wasn't. I really did believe Bob and I could handle them. In my opinion, the Thorndyke boys were basically cowards. In all the killing they'd done, they always had an advantage. Whenever I'd directly confronted them in the past, they folded up real quick. If Bob and I could catch them off guard from two sides, I was pretty sure they'd surrender without a fight.

We heard the train whistle as we approached the station. As the train came chugging to a stop, we stepped up onto the platform. Lora, Becky, and the kids were down at the other end. We waved at each other. I could see the kids were fascinated by the train with all the smoke, noise, and steam.

The conductor stepped off, followed by a couple of passengers.

Tom and I joined Lora and Becky with the kids at the far end of the platform, taking a moment to watch the passengers getting on and off. One of the men who had gotten off the train caught my eye. There was something about his body language. He didn't seem to have a particular destination in mind.

Lora and I said goodbye to Tom and Becky and started back the way Tom and I had come across the platform. As we passed the man I'd noticed earlier, I noticed he was wearing a gun in a tied down holster.

I leaned into Lora's ear.

"Take the kids and go straight to the livery stable. The team is hitched and ready to go. I'll be along in a minute. I think there might be a problem here."

She shot me a worried look. I smiled in a way that I hoped would be reassuring.

"I'll catch up to you in minute,"

I turned back toward the man.

Tom saw me, and I caught his eye, glancing over toward the man with the tied down gun, whom I could now see was pretty young—maybe twenty years old or so.

I approached the man straight on.

"Howdy, you look like you might be lost."

He grinned, a kind of one-sided, crooked grin.

"Are you from around here?" he asked.

"Yes, sir, I am. Can I help you?"

"I'm looking for a man named Wes Spradlin. Have you heard of him?"

Tom had left Becky's side and was coming toward us.

"Yes, I sure have. He lives right here in town, mister... ?"

"I'm Luke Watson. Maybe you've heard of me?"

I shook my head.

"Watson is a pretty common name, I guess. Say, Mr. Watson, that sure is a fancy gun rig you have there."

He narrowed his eyes, with a sneer on his face

"What's it to you?"

"Me? Oh, nothing really. It's just that there's a city ordinance against carrying handguns in town."

Tom had stopped about ten feet directly behind the man.

"Don't mean shit to me. Where does Wes Spradlin live?"

"Why do you want to see him?"

"That's none of your damned business."

"Actually, it is," I said, as I opened my jacket with my left hand so he could see both my badge and my gun.

He spread his legs and put his hand above his gun.

"I said it ain't. Are you feeling lucky?"

That's when Tom hit him. Tom had drawn his gun and taken two quick steps up behind Watson. Watson sensed Tom's approach and started to draw and turn at the same time. Tom's gun barrel came down on Watson's head. He collapsed like somebody had let all the air out of him.

"That was smooth, Tom, very smooth," I said.

Tom tossed me the man's gun.

"Yeah, well he had it coming,"

Tom handcuffed the man's wrists together behind his back. He frisked the man thoroughly, and came up with a knife and a derringer, both of which he dropped into a pocket of his uniform jacket.

I examined the man's revolver. It was a new model Colt, chambered in .44 caliber. It had five notches filed into the grip, a tin horn trademark.

Watson was waking up as Becky approached.

"Becky, honey, I've got to take this fella down to the jail. Would you mind going to the house alone. I'll come along and have my lunch in thirty minutes or so."

Becky nodded.

"Okay, I'll see you there."

She turned and walked away.

Watson sat up.

"What'd you hit me for?" he asked.

"You're under arrest for unlawfully carrying a handgun within the city limits of Bear Creek, failure to surrender your weapon, attempted assault on a peace officer, and whatever else I can think up between here and the jail," Tom said, hauling Watson to his feet.

"I'll see you, John. You be real careful up there in North Fork,"

I handed over Watson's gun and watched Tom march him away.

I found myself smiling.

Tom hadn't lost his edge.

Dan Arnold

29.

As we drove down the hill from the center of town, Wes Spradlin's buggy was parked in front of the house, near Bob's horse where it stood tied at the hitching rail.

"So much for lunch alone with the family." I thought.

I dropped Lora and the kids near the house and drove the team down to the barn. As I was unharnessing the horses, Wes and Bob came out to join me.

"Have you seen the storm up there in the mountains? It appears to be headed this way," Bob said.

"Yeah, we're gonna catch bad weather either here or there," I replied.

"You're both welcome to ride in the buggy with me." Wes offered. "It will keep most of the rain off us."

"Thank you, no. I have my slicker, I'll be fine." Bob replied.

"I was planning to ride with you anyway, Wes. Thanks," I said.

Bob and Wes turned the horses out into the pasture while I hung the harness on the pegs.

"Can I offer you boys a late lunch?" I said.

Bob grinned.

"I timed my arrival a bit before the scheduled appointment in the hopes I would be invited," He said.

Wes nodded with a chuckle.

"Yeah, me, too."

* * *

By the time we finished at the barn, the children had eaten and were playing in the yard. Lora, Wes, Bob and I found ourselves thrown together. Not exactly the "family" meal I had hoped for.

While the conversation was congenial, it was a little bit rushed, and there was an underlying tension. Lora was not her usual smiling and gracious self. As we wolfed down the delicious meal Consuela had prepared, we talked about the weather and events in town. It was strange there were only four of us at the table. Until recently, there'd always been a full dining room at lunch time. The current situation was not clear to either Lora or me. Lora wanted to take in boarders. While I wasn't comfortable with the notion, I'd agreed to see how it worked out.

We were still at the table when there was knock on the door. Consuela answered it, and brought a heavy set man into the dining room. Introductions were made all around. The man was named Tony Morgan. He was moving here from Iowa, and he was considering opening a furniture and appliance business in Bear Creek. He figured to be in the area for a week or so. We invited him to sit and eat. Someone in town had recommended he look into lodging here.

"Well, I had a late breakfast in town, but I never turn down the offer of a home cooked meal," he said.

Bob and Wes excused themselves, and I took a moment to be alone with Lora while Consuela served the guest.

I wrapped her in my arms.

"I'll be back tomorrow, first thing. I'll come straight home." I told her.

"Promise me, John," she said, searching my eyes.

"Of course, but I can't be sure what time I'll get back."

"No. Promise me that you really are coming back."

"Baby girl, I promise I'll come home to you as fast as I can, unless God has other plans."

She closed her eyes and took a long slow breath.

"That's good enough for me. I'll be praying every minute you're gone. Don't take any chances, darling. If it comes down to you or them . . . ."

"I understand. I love you."

***

We loaded our gear into the buggy Wes was driving. Bob, wrapped in his slicker was riding his high stepping black horse. Wes and I were both wearing our slickers as well, though we were riding in the buggy. We could see the rain clouds descending out of the mountains, but the three of us were dry and in the sunshine for the time being.

"When we get to North Fork, I plan to head straight into town and start hitting the saloons," Bob started. "How do you boys want to handle it?"

"I expect Wes and I'll go straight to the property we want to look at, and then we'll meet you at whatever time and place we agree on."

"Where would that be? I've never been up to North Fork."

I'd been giving it some thought.

"As we come into town, the livery stable is on the left, and it's the first thing you come to on the road as you're going into North Fork. It's about a block from the first saloon which is called the Jubilee House. I think we should meet in the barn, especially if it's still raining up there."

"Where is this property you gentlemen are so bent on inspecting?"

"It's a large white house, right by the creek and about two blocks southwest of the main street. It sits on twenty five acres along the creek, so we'll probably be able to see it as we head into town. We have to go right through the main part of North Fork before we take the lane over to the property. Like I said, I think we'll drive straight there rather than stopping at the livery stable."

Bob looked worried.

"What's troubling you, Bob?"

"This entire plan hinges on us having the element of surprise. We have to be able to get the drop on those men before they have any idea they are even in jeopardy. To me, going right through the middle of town just so you can look at a house seems like an unnecessary risk."

"Not really. First of all, we left later than planned, so by the time we get there it'll be almost dark—it might even be raining. Second, I'm the only one of the three of us that anyone up there would recognize. When we go through town, I'll pull down my hat and slump over in the buggy like I'm drunk or asleep. It's a pretty common sight up there."

"Really, play acting? That's the best answer you have? What do you think, preacher man?"

Wes considered his reply.

"I think it is all in God's hands. Perhaps we could take a moment to pray together."

Bob snorted in disdain.

"No offense, Parson, but perhaps you haven't heard. There is a noted German theologian who has confirmed the death of God. It seems that after God created the universe, He died and left things spinning along all on their own. I am not about to waste my time praying to some dead God who can do nothing to help me in my present misery. I trust in Samuel Colt, Sharps, and Winchester, not God."

To my surprise, Wes just smiled!

"Well, Bob, as it happens I am quite familiar with the writings of Friedrich Nietzsche. He is more of a philosopher and philologist than a theologian. He may also be quite insane. I know for a fact he is a bit too fond of the poppy. His work and influence was a topic of some research and discussion while I was at Seminary."

"Well, Reverend, it seems to me, Mr. Nietzsche's focus has been on having an open mind and seeking the truth, especially as it is found in science, even when it is inconvenient to religion."

I had no idea Bob was such a reader.

"So then, Bob, if I understand you correctly, you're saying you believe in Truth with a capital 'T.' Is that correct?"

Bob thought about it for a moment. I think he knew he was in trouble.

"I'm saying the search for truth, whatever it may be, is vastly more important than a foolish belief in fairy tales and mysticism."

"I quite agree with you there, Bob..." Wes said.

Bob glanced at him quickly.

Wes didn't acknowledge Bob's surprised look. He just went on with his explanation.

"The search for Truth is what eventually brought me to the Bible. I read it with an open mind and a fair amount of skepticism. I found the Truth, or maybe the Truth found me. Tell me, Bob, are you a student of the Bible?"

"Hell, no! Oh, I've read it some, and I've heard plenty of preachers talk about it. It's not for me, Preacher."

"Then you are in no position to talk about having either an open mind or a sincere search for Truth—are you, Bob?"

We rode along in silence for a while.

Occasionally, we met a rider or wagon coming down out of the mountains. They appeared to be hurrying to get away from the storm, the same storm we were riding directly up into.

We could see the edge of the rain a couple of miles away. The thunderhead was a huge column of cloud, thousands of feet high, illuminated in several colors by the setting sun and the occasional flash of lightening from within. Thunder boomed occasionally.

***

I hated to bring it up, but Wes had to know.

"Wes, I was over at the railroad depot when the 12:10 to Denver came in. A man got off the train looking for you."

Wes just waited for me to go on.

"He had a tied down gun with five notches on the grip."

Wes took a deep breath and let it out slowly.

"Does the gentleman have a name?"

"He said his name is Luke Watson. He's young, maybe twenty or so. Do you know him?"

Wes thought for a moment.

"No. Not that I recall. Watson is a pretty common name. Did he indicate why he was looking for me?"

"No, but he was on the prod and itching for a gun fight."

"Where is he now?"

"He's in the city jail. Tom bent a gun barrel over his head to keep him from pulling his pistol on one of us."

Wes looked relieved.

"Only a two bit punk carves notches in his gun," Bob said.

Wes nodded in agreement.

"I've never been proud of the killing I've done. Even when I was a proud and wicked man, I always felt bad about killing someone. I killed a man once for just spilling my drink. I was paid to fight, and I was willing to do it, but I never celebrated killing anyone."

"Was it always a fair fight?"

"No, not really—it wasn't. Sometimes, it was practically murder. The man I killed for spilling a drink was no gun fighter. I challenged him in front of all his friends. I was very drunk, but, still, there was no way he was going to get a bullet into me. I wish he hadn't felt like he had to try. I shamed him into it. He reached for his gun, and I shot him before he ever cleared the holster."

Bob looked at him.

"What about now, Reverend?"

"Now, I regret every aspect of the life I used to lead."

"That's not what I was enquiring about. What I meant to ask you was this; could you still kill someone if you had to?"

Wes looked over at Bob.

"I no longer look for trouble. I try to avoid it and live at peace with all men. If that isn't possible, I'll do what I have to do. Sometimes trouble comes looking for you."

"Amen, Preacher, it does for a fact!" Bob said.

I was reminded, for some men; Bob was the trouble that came looking for them.

Wes looked at me.

"I've been expecting something like this, John," he said quietly. "They'll keep coming, you know."

I nodded.

"The wages of sin is death," I thought.

Dan Arnold

30.

Riding into the rain was like the difference between day and night. It started with just a few giant drops of water popping the dust on both the buggy and the road. Suddenly it was a deluge. Thunder growled and crashed, and lightening flashed and flared. The sound of the rain alone drowned out any hope of further conversation. In the tremendous downpour, Bob and his horse were only a few feet off to my side and they nearly disappeared from my sight.

We probably traveled a couple of miles before the rain began to soften to a steady downpour. Great sheets and currents of water ran down the road cutting channels and furrows in the surface.

I felt sorry for our horses. Slipping and sliding, with their ears down, cold rainwater just streaming off them. They plodded on, though, splashing through the mud and the streams of runoff water.

All three of us humans were pretty well soaked and miserable ourselves. Even in the buggy, there wasn't much cover, so the rain blew in. When we were going up steep slopes, the buggy offered no protection at all.

Eventually, we topped out on a ridge and had a partial view of North Fork in its little hanging valley. Seen through the distorting curtains of rain, it looked as though all of the lamps were lit in the town. It looked warm and inviting.

Coming out of the forest on the outskirts of North Fork, the rain had softened to a heavy mist and the temperature had dropped by at least twenty degrees. The heavy cloud cover and mist made it seem like a perpetual twilight, nearly as dark as full nightfall. It was murky, and everything was softened as though we were in a cloud, which I guess we were. Water was gently dripping off the spruce and aspen trees, the buildings, and pretty much every surface in sight.

The street wasn't deserted, though. Several horses and mules stood tied to hitching rails with their heads down. Occasionally, someone could be seen splashing through the mud, hopping over runoff as they crossed the main street.

"Bob, let's meet in the barn at the livery stable at about seven o'clock. By then, you may have seen them. If not, you and Wes can start looking for them together or split up, whichever you prefer."

"That's only about an hour from now. Will it give you enough time to look over the house and land?"

"Yeah, I expect so. We'll see you then."

Wes slapped the reins, and the horse stepped up into a trot. We left Bob walking his horse up the street as we approached the Jubilee House.

**

Even this early in the evening, Tommy Turner's Jubilee House was well-lit and so were most of the customers we could see through the windows as we went by.

The place appeared to have plenty of patrons.

There was loud laughter and hoots and hollers coming from inside. Piano music was being pounded out by a partially-impaired musician battering away on an out-of-tune instrument.

That noise flowed right into the mix, coming from the two saloons on opposite corners, where we turned left on the lane which eventually led down to the house by the creek.

The Gold Dust Hotel and Casino had their own piano player hammering away, as did the Oxbow Hotel and Saloon. I noticed much less laughter and no hooting coming from those places. Peering through the windows of the Oxbow, we caught a glimpse of some dancing girls on a stage. We could smell the stink of unwashed bodies, cheap whisky, and tobacco smoke as we went between those buildings. Moments before, we had been enjoying the crisp mountain air, scrubbed clean by the passing storm. From now on, we would enjoy nothing North Fork had to offer.

We needn't have worried about being recognized. No one even seemed to notice us passing through. Nearly everyone was inside somewhere drinking, gambling, or just generally carousing. The few people we saw outside were typical hard-working men on their way to or from one of those saloons, or relieving themselves, off the boardwalk right into the street.

There were no guns in sight. That was Tommy Turner's policy, and he enforced it. It didn't mean there were no guns being carried by patrons or others; it just meant there were fewer gun fights in town. I'd seen the high chair where Tommy put his man with a shotgun, to keep everybody honest and peaceable in the Jubilee House. That would be true in the other gambling halls as well. Nobody wanted to cheat, steal, or start trouble with a double-barreled, eight gauge shotgun hovering above them.

***

The lane ended in a wide area with hitching rails and places to park buggies. There was only a single horse tied, and ours was the only buggy, so far this evening.

There was a picket fence around the house. The front gate had an arbor arch with a sign on it. The sign had fancy flowing script that simply read "Aphrodite's Bower."

The house was quite large, two stories tall with three gables on each side of the roof. There were chimneys at each end. The building was built of wood, whitewashed, and well-lit inside and out. There was no loud music or laughter to be heard.

Lace curtains covered all the windows.

We sat in the buggy for a moment and considered the property.

It was a good two blocks away from the main street of North Fork, and, from here, you could barely hear the racket coming from the bawdy houses.

The house was flanked by a carriage house and three separate outhouses.

Somewhere beyond our sight, we could hear the north fork of Bear Creek, cascading over the rocks and rills,

"This could work as an orphanage, if the town wasn't so horrible," Wes observed.

"Well, that's about to change. This will be a different place in a few more weeks."

Wes nodded.

"I'd like to see a church built right here on the side of this lane—a big white church with a tall steeple. It would be the first thing you saw when you looked at the town."

I could see him visualizing it, as he spread his hands wide.

"A church would need a preacher," I said, as I stepped out of the buggy.

He looked at me and winked.

"Why, yes it would." He said.

***

On the porch, we shook off some of the rain water, while we surveyed as much of the land as we could see.

"There's plenty of room here for youngsters to play, even enough room for some livestock. They could have a milk cow, chickens, and what not. They could even have a garden," Wes said.

"Good grass and water," I added.

"She is generous, isn't she?"

I knew Wes was referring to Mrs. Poole.

"More than most people will ever know," I said.

I knocked on the front door.

It was answered by a huge black man.

When I say huge, I mean he filled the doorway. That man was well over six feet tall and at least three feet wide. His arms were bigger than my legs. He was as dark as I have ever seen any man, which just made his big white smile seem even brighter.

He was dressed in a tailored suit. When he spoke, his voice made me think of thick smoke rolling across open water.

"Good evening, gentlemen. Ah'm Maximilian Beauregard. Y'all can call me Max. May I see yo invitations?"

Wes and I looked at each other and then up into Max's smiling face. "Uh, we don't have any invitations," I said.

Max frowned. It was intimidating.

Wes and I took an involuntary step back.

"Ah'm afraid ah'wl hafta ask y'all to leave. This heah establishment is by invitation only."

Wes and I looked at each other again.

"We were invited by Mrs. Poole, but she didn't give us printed invitations," I said.

His smile came back and lit up his whole face.

"Well, that's fine then, just fine. Is she expecting y'all?"

We heard a feminine voice call out. "Who is it, Max?"

I recognized it as being Mrs. Poole's voice. Apparently, so did Wes.

He looked suddenly ill.

The big Black man looked down at us.

"They didn't say, but I reckon they is the law," he growled.

"Well then, by all means let them in, Max," Mrs. Poole said.

Dan Arnold

31.

Wes and I removed our soggy hats and stepped into the foyer of the house, mindful of our wet slickers and muddy boots. The foyer was in the middle of the first floor with a split staircase on the far side of the room. With the exception of the polished oak floor, all the visible wood was dark walnut and polished with care. The runner on the staircase appeared to be oriental and the lamps were all crystal. The whole effect was elegant.

There was a doorway to our right that might lead back to the kitchen. To our left was a sitting room in which four women were sitting on velvet covered chairs and an ottoman. All the furniture was upholstered in green velvet, the color of emeralds.

One of the women was holding a violin in her lap.

"May ah take yo hats and coats," Max asked, though it sounded more like a command.

We shrugged out of our slickers. Max hung them and our hats on a coat rack by the front door.

I saw him eyeing our guns. I was shocked to see Wes was wearing a tied down gun under his slicker. I couldn't figure out when he could have put it on, or why he had done so. I noticed he wasn't wearing his clerical collar either.

"This way, gentlemen." Max said, sweeping his arm toward the sitting room.

As we stepped into the sitting room, Mrs. Poole's jaw dropped and she paled visibly.

"Wes, is that you?"

Quietly, he replied.

"Yes, Emma, it's me."

Quickly recovering her poise, she offered me her hand.

"Good evening, Sheriff Sage. May I introduce you to these ladies?"

"A pleasure, I'm sure," I said, immediately regretting my choice of words.

There were smiles all around the room except for myself and Wes. I was completely chagrined, and Wes had his eyes closed trying to pretend he hadn't heard me say it.

"Sheriff Sage, this is Nancy, Debbie, and Victoria. Debbie has been playing her violin for us. Ladies, may I introduce John Everett Sage, the Sheriff of this county."

Various pleasantries were mumbled in response.

While I was aware we were in a house of ill repute, the women were all fashionably dressed and could've been mistaken for ladies of high society. In my experience, it was an uncommon thing among working girls.

Mrs. Poole was not about to forget her manners.

"Ladies, may I introduce an old friend, Mr. Wesley Spradlin. I have no idea why he is here. Indeed, why are you here Mr. Spradlin?"

Wes opened his mouth, but no words came out. He closed his mouth and looked quickly at me.

"Mr. Spradlin is the interim pastor of our church in Bear Creek. He is also going to be leading the committee to establish a county orphanage."

Mrs. Poole blinked several times. It appeared she would've been less surprised if I'd said Wes was a traveling clown.

Again, she recovered quickly.

"Oh my, I've completely forgotten my manners! Gentlemen, please have a seat. May I offer you some refreshment? It's a nasty night out, what with the storm and all."

"No, thank you, Ma'am," I replied.

"Nonsense, I insist! Max, please go to the kitchen, and ask Ophelia to send in some coffee and sandwiches. Thank you."

"Yes'm," Max said.

With a little bow, he turned and left the room.

"Gentlemen, please be seated," she repeated.

We found seats on the other side of the room. We found ourselves sitting on velvet covered chairs on opposite sides of a grand piano. I was acutely aware of my muddy boots and wet clothing.

Debbie put her violin into a case.

Mrs. Poole took the opportunity to get straight to the point.

"Ladies, as you know the Sheriff here is the reason we are going out of business at this address. As I told you, I've promised this building and the land for the establishment of an orphanage and school. You may have heard that the Sheriff is going to clean up this town. He has my full support and confidence."

I found her comments to be both gracious and surprising. I'd had no idea we would even see her in North Fork.

"Thank you, Mrs. Poole. I must say finding you up here comes as something of a surprise."

"I came up on Saturday to begin addressing the issues of closing this business. As of today, we are effectively out of business. I've contracted with Atwater Freight to move the furniture and fixtures to Denver. I expect to have the move completed by the end of the week, and the buildings will be available starting next week. Does this meet with your approval?"

"Yes, Ma'am, it surely does. It's a pretty clear indicator; things are changing in North Fork. Have you experienced any opposition?"

"Not yet. This is the first day we are out of business. We've turned away three prospective clients this evening, and I expect the word is getting around town.

We've always catered to, shall we say, a more sophisticated clientele. We have visitors from all over the Front Range, even from as far away as Denver and Cheyenne. Of course, much of our business comes from Bear Creek. We've been a bit more expensive than other establishments in this town, which allows us to be somewhat choosier about our clientele, while still operating at a reasonable profit."

I put my finger tips together.

"I can see you're a canny, clever, and discrete business woman, Mrs. Poole. Until you came to my office, I thought you were retired."

She smiled.

"I established this business before I sold my interests in the town of Waller to Spencer Wilson, the so called 'mayor' of that town."

I nodded.

"I'm glad you've arranged to complete the move quickly. There could be trouble from some of the locals."

She waved a hand dismissively.

"I can take care of myself. Speaking of trouble," she turned to Wes, "are you really a preacher? You sure don't look like one."

Wes smiled and bowed slightly.

"If this evening proves anything, it is that appearances can be deceiving. I'm here in both my capacity as a minister and in my capacity as a friend of the Sheriff."

Before she could ask about that, Max returned with a cart upon which were a china coffee pot, several cups on saucers, a little pitcher of cream, and a plate stacked with sandwiches.

Seeing Max, pushing that cart, reminded me of a locomotive pushing a baby carriage.

There was a knock on the front door.

"If all y'all will excuse me, ah'll just go see who that is," Max said.

"Thank you, Max, we can manage from here," Mrs. Poole replied.

After he left the room, I commented, "Max seems like a man who could sort out any unsavory types."

"Oh, yes, he can. We do not allow anyone to bring guns into this house, and anyone who would try to quarrel with Max would regret it—if they survived."

"You're fortunate to have him, Emma," Wes agreed. "Sometime, I would like to hear the story of how you were able to obtain his services."

"Perhaps, sometime I'll have occasion to tell you, Wes," she replied.

Mrs. Poole poured coffee while Victoria offered us sandwiches.

Max came back into the room.

"Who was that, Max?" Mrs. Poole asked.

"Young gentleman, had him an invitation, gone now," Max said.

"Thank you, Max."

He bowed his head.

"Emma, you mentioned you didn't allow guns in this house. I apologize for coming in here armed." I said.

She shrugged.

I looked at Max.

"Why didn't you take our guns, Max?"

"Got to allow for the law," he said. "Sides, y'all don't figure to disarm easy."

"I think you could probably disarm a grizzly bear," I said.

He chuckled.

"Naw'suh, ah'd rather not, but, if'n ah had it to do, ah would sho'nuff try."

I believed him.

***

After a bit, Mrs. Poole offered us a tour of the house.

Downstairs, we'd already seen the sitting room. We also found a library, dining room, pantry, and kitchen. We met Ophelia in the kitchen. She was, or had been, the cook and maid for the establishment.

Upstairs, were six bedrooms, two on each side of a central hallway at the top of the stairs, two more at each end.

"This house is perfect," Wes said. "We could have up to four kids per room. That would allow for twenty, leaving one room for a couple to manage the place. If we convert the library into a bed room downstairs, we could house up to twenty four kids here."

I could see that, but I was thinking beyond the facility.

"It means hiring a couple to manage the place, and someone would have to help with the cooking and cleaning. The original plan was for volunteers from Bear Creek to handle those duties. North Fork is too far away for volunteers from Bear Creek to be reliable."

"I can help find suitable people right here in North Fork," Mrs. Poole said.

"Could you, Emma?" Wes asked.

"Oh, yes, don't forget there are a number of people up here about to become unemployed. Don't worry; some of them are very fine people, respectable enough even for the church ladies."

It was Ophelia's turn to speak up.

"I believe I would like to stay on here. I'm a very good cook, and nobody can do laundry better'n me. I'm sorry, Miz Emma, but I don't wanna move to Denver, and I never did like working in no cat house, no offense intended, ma'am. My man and me got us a nice little house here, and we sure do want to stay."

"I'm not offended. Oh, my! Well, if it can be arranged, you are welcome to stay, Ophelia. I'll have a difficult time trying to replace you, though."

Wes was thinking things over.

"You know something, John, if the churches would all pitch in some money every month, we'd be able to pay the salary for the staff and the food for the kids. Then the county wouldn't have to come up with much funding. I believe we can make them see the sense in that. Alta Vista County would only bear the cost of some essential maintenance and repairs."

I nodded, looking at my watch.

"Mrs. Poole, if you'll excuse us, we have some business to attend to. It's time for us to go."

"Certainly, gentlemen, it was lovely to see you— especially you, Wes—or should I call you reverend?"

"I'm Wes, Emma—please, just Wes. I'll always be Wes to you."

She smiled and said, "I'll look forward to seeing you again soon then, Wes."

"Will we see you back in Bear Creek, Mrs. Poole?" I asked.

"Oh yes. I have yet to draw up the papers and the agreement to present to the county. I'll try to have it done this week or next. I still have my home in Bear Creek.

Debbie will manage my business interests in Denver, with Max's assistance. I can catch the train and run down there whenever I want to. I'm not planning to move any time soon."

When she said that last part, she was looking at Wes.

Dan Arnold

32.

We climbed back in the buggy and headed for the livery stable. As we approached the corner between the Gold Dust and the Oxbow, a man was walking across the street, on his way into the Gold Dust Hotel and Casino. When he glanced at us, I recognized him as being none other than Tommy Turner, the Sheriff of North Fork. He didn't give us a second look, so I figured he hadn't recognized me in my soggy hat and slicker, one of two men riding in a buggy.

When we pulled up at the livery stable, I had Wes help me carry the box with our gear into the barn. I lit a lamp so we could see. He took out his pocket watch.

"It's just after seven o'clock, John. What's our next move?"

I opened the box and brought out two shotguns and the box of 12 gauge shells.

"What is that?" Wes asked, eyeing my brand new Winchester lever action shotgun.

"A Mormon friend of mine over in Utah, by the name of John Browning, designed this for Winchester. It holds five 12 gauge shells instead of the usual one or two. Works just like a lever action rifle. He sent it to me as a present when I got elected sheriff.

Wes nodded his appreciation.

"Now that the rain has stopped, people are starting to move around."

"I saw the local sheriff going into the Gold Dust. His name is Tommy Turner. I'd like to talk to him…" I started.

"That would be a wise move," Bob said, as he stepped forward out of the shadows at the back of the barn.

"Whoa, John, it's just me."

I realized I had my .45 cocked and aimed right at him. I hadn't even thought about it. Wes gave me an appraising look, as I holstered the Colt.

"That was not your smartest moment, Bob," I growled.

"No, apparently it was not. You have my sincere apologies and my thanks. Thank you for allowing me to continue living my life, so I may reflect on my error. And thank you for not firing your gun, thereby raising an alarm."

I was half tempted to shoot him anyway.

"As I was saying, I want to talk to Tommy Turner, but I can't go to him, so he'll have to come to me. Would one of you gentlemen be good enough to go fetch him down here?"

Bob held a hand up and interrupted again.

"Before we get the local law involved, and as I said, I agree it's a good idea, we need to get something straight," he said.

"And that is?"

"What exactly is our intention toward the miscreants we are hunting?"

"We find them and arrest them. Then we haul them back to Bear Creek to stand trial."

"I disagree."

"You what?"

"I disagree, John. I believe the order of ceremonies should be as follows."

He started counting off on his black gloved fingers.

"We locate the men in question. We kill the men in question. Then we go home happy, and may I add, healthy."

He smiled, holding up three fingers.

I was aware of how intently Wes was watching this exchange.

"We've talked about this, Bob. We're here to enforce the law. I won't do murder." I said.

"I fully understand our duty under the law, John. I would not suggest such a thing.

However, since you bring up the subject of murder, I would point out the Thorndykes intend to murder you, upon their first opportunity. My thought was to engage them in mortal combat, intended to culminate with a satisfactory conclusion, thus preventing them from murdering you."

I was thinking, *"Why does Bob always use twenty words when five would do?"*

I shook it off.

"I don't expect they'll give us cause, Bob. The Thorndykes are cowards. They never beat anybody in a straight up fight, never even tried it. They always make sure they have the advantage over their victims. They may be murderers, but they aren't warriors. They won't want any part of a real fight. When we brace them, I expect they'll fold up like a ladies' fan. Justice will be done."

Bob shrugged.

Wes spoke up.

"And what does the Lord require of you? A man should do justice, love mercy, and walk humbly with his God," He quoted from the scripture. "While these outlaws you're after do not seem to be men of that type, I hope *we* are,"

Bob didn't like it

"Maybe *you* are, preacher, but you don't speak for me. I believe tonight some lives will be required. I don't intend to let mine will be one of them. Further, I observe you have chosen to arm yourself. It seems to me a tied down gun is hardly appropriate for a meek and lowly preacher. Apparently you have no intention of turning the other cheek."

Wes nodded.

"Perhaps you should think of me as a work in progress, Bob,"

I stepped between them.

"I still need someone to go get Sheriff Turner from the Gold Dust, without attracting any attention,"

"I'll go. I was able to observe the gentleman while I was at the Jubilee House earlier," Bob said.

I glanced at Bob.

"I guess you didn't see the Thorndykes there?"

He shook his head.

"Be careful. We don't want anyone but Sheriff Turner to know we're here—or why,"

After Bob disappeared into the night, Wes again suggested we should pray.

So, we did.

It was nearly thirty minutes before the barn door slid open again.

Sheriff Tommy Turner stepped in, followed by Bob.

"What is this about, Sage?" Tommy demanded, "Why all the secrecy?"

"Hello, Tommy. I see you've met Bob, let me introduce Wes Spradlin. Wes, this is Tommy Turner, the sheriff of North Fork."

Meeting the famous gunman was unnerving to Tommy. It showed on his face.

"What the hell is going on?" Was all he could manage to sputter.

"Tommy, we have reason to believe the men who robbed the bank in Bear Creek are here in North Fork. We're looking for four men who would have come into town yesterday. Did you happen to notice four rough-looking, armed men come into town yesterday?"

He looked at each of us, and what he saw on our faces convinced him to tell the truth.

"Yeah, I know the men you're talking about. You know I don't allow the carrying of guns in town. Those boys came into town and went straight to the Gold

Dust. I didn't see them come in, but one of my men told me four men carrying guns were over there."

"Are they still there?" I asked.

"I saw Henry and Harvey in the saloon at the Gold Dust, John," Bob stated. "I didn't see Homer, though, and I don't know for sure what the fourth man, Tom Russel, looks like. He may be with Homer somewhere. They could be upstairs with a couple of women or over at the Oxbow. We haven't looked in there yet."

"Yeah, two of um are still in the Gold Dust," Tommy confirmed.

"Are they still armed, Tommy?"

Tommy nodded.

"Yeah, seems like they struck up a friendship with Ian McGregger. He owns the place. I don't interfere in his business. When I went over there to see about those men and take their guns, Ian waved me off."

"You let them keep their guns because this guy, McGregger, said so?"

Tommy nodded again.

"My men carry guns; he has men with guns. We need um to keep people honest. You probably want to keep your guns, right?"

Bob looked disgusted.

"How many armed men does McGregger have over there, Tommy?" I asked.

He shrugged.

"Maybe a couple of men working security for him. He has a lookout with a shotgun sitting up on the landing. He can see the whole saloon from there."

I looked at Bob for confirmation.

"That is correct. He was the only lookout I observed. I believe there are other armed men in the saloon, I was unable to see their weapons."

"Tommy, we're going to need your help. Can you get a deputy or one of your men to join us?"

Tommy shook his head.

"Uh, uh. You've got no friends in this town. I won't mix in. You'll have to skin your own cats."

"What kind of sheriff are you?" Wes asked.

"I live here, and I'm part of the business community. I can't take sides in something like this. I'll do you the same courtesy. I won't back you, and I won't back them none either."

Wes, Bob, and I looked at each other.

"Tommy, you're some piece of work. I can't imagine what would've happened if you'd been elected instead of me." I said.

"Things would be better for everybody. If you get into a fight with McGregger and he wins, I win. If you beat him, that's good for me too. Hell, I stand to win either way. With any luck, you'll get yourself killed tonight. That would solve a bunch of my problems."

I chuckled at that.

"You should be so lucky, Tommy. I'll tell you this, if you don't have my back in this, you're no lawman."

"I'm all the law we need in North Fork."

"Maybe," Bob started, "but you'd better keep your mouth closed. If I see your face on the wrong side tonight, Turner, this town will be short one sheriff."

Tommy looked at him and back peddled for the door.

"Now, hold on. I told you I would stay out of it, and I will. I sure will."

"Go find a hole to hide in Tommy," I said, as he quickly disappeared from sight.

"Now what will we do?" Wes asked.

"Nothing's changed. I didn't really expect any help from our friend, Sheriff Turner. I was just hoping he was a better man—my mistake. At least now we know where two of the Thorndykes are. Bob, I want you to go over to the Oxbow and have a look around. See if Homer and Russel are over there."

"Certainly; however, if they are in that location we have a problem. We can't afford to divide our forces, and we cannot be in two places at the same time."

I nodded.

"We'll cross that bridge when we come to it."

33.

Bob came back with a negative report. The missing men were not at the Oxbow.

"Okay, we have to decide whether to wait for Russel and Homer to show up, or take Henry and Harvey right now, since we know where they are. I'm open to suggestions."

"I suggest we formulate a plan of attack and take those two while we can. The other two won't be nearly as much of a threat as having all four of them gunning for you," Bob said.

"Agreed; it's better to get two than none. We need to have a plan in place in the event the other two show up unexpectedly. We need to figure out how best to neutralize the shotgun lookout and get the drop on Harvey and Henry. Our timing has to be perfect."

Bob nodded.

"I checked out the Gold Dust pretty thoroughly. That guy with the shotgun is focused on the gamblers down on the main floor. He's sitting in a chair on the landing between the saloon and the hotel rooms. There is some traffic going up and down those stairs. I can get into the hotel by climbing up the back stairs on the outside of the building. I'll come down the hall and approach the lookout from behind him. He won't expect to be attacked at all. I'll take him out and be in a position to see the whole ground floor. The Thorndyke boys are in a poker game with Martin Pogue, at a table very near the staircase. I'll be right above them."

That was a good plan.

"Excellent! Our odds of success are greatly improved by the fact there are only two of them in there. Again though, timing is everything. We both need to brace them at the same time, you from above them and me from the ground floor."

"I can help with that," Wes interjected, holding up his watch. "It's almost eight fifteen now; let's plan to hit them at eight forty five. We'll go up to the Gold Dust together, but I'll be the only one to go inside. I'll walk in the front and take a quick look around. If everything is still the way Bob described it, I'll stay inside somewhere where I can be seen from the door. If something has changed, I'll come right back outside and we'll go somewhere and re-evaluate. If I do stay inside, Bob you'll need to go get into position to take out the lookout. I'll be watching for you. The minute you move to hit him, I'll signal John to come on in."

Having Wes with us was a real advantage.

"I like it. I'll stay on the porch right outside those swinging doors. There's plenty of light there, so my eyes won't have to adjust to a sudden change when I come through the doors. I'll be able to see some of the room before I come in," I said.

"Reverend, you don't want to go walking in there with your handgun showing. That will attract too much attention," Bob said.

"Actually, I'll be wearing my slicker, so it won't show. I'll look pretty much the same as anybody else coming in out of the weather. I intend to attract some attention though, right when you go to hit the lookout. When I move, it will distract the lookout and be the signal for John to come in."

Bob grinned.

"This tactic has an excellent chance of being successful. It's early on a rainy, Monday night. It's certain no one will be expecting this kind of drama. We can approach under cover of darkness and hide our shotguns under our slickers. We'll hit them fast and from two different directions, catching them sitting down. They won't know whether to fiddle or fart. Yes, I like it as well."

***

We reached the Gold Dust without incident. Bob went down the side of the building to wait for my signal. Wes walked straight in the swinging doors. I watched him from outside as he stopped for a moment and gave the room a quick scan. Just like anyone would do. Several people gave him a look and then went back to minding their own business. Wes nodded slightly and headed toward the bar. I moved to where I could just barely see him. He was speaking to the bartender. After a minute or so, I saw the bartender hand him a beer. I signaled for Bob to go up the back stairs.

I looked at my watch. It was eight forty.

From where I was on the porch, I could see the lookout sitting in his chair on the landing. I thought I could also see where the Thorndyke's were sitting. Wes had stayed over near the bar. That hadn't been the original plan, but Wes understood I could see the lookout from where I was. Wes was actually in a better place, being by the bar, because whatever he was planning to do to get attention would distract the lookout from seeing me coming through the doors.

I wasn't happy with the number of people milling about in the saloon. There were three or four scantily clad women flirting with customers. Some men were throwing dice over in a corner and another group were at a roulette wheel. Those people were all standing.

There were at least three tables with people playing poker, faro, or some other card game. All together there were now about thirty customers in the building and some of them were moving about.

A waiter delivered drinks from the bar. The piano player was busy making his idea of music, and the conversation level was strident as people tried to talk loud enough to be heard over the piano and the general din of noise.

Bob appeared at the top of the stairs.

As he came down the stairs, he brought the double barreled shotgun out from under his slicker.

"Nobody move!" Wes yelled, sweeping his slicker aside and revealing his tied down gun. Heads whipped around to look at him, including the lookout, but everybody froze for just a second.

Bob slammed the butt of his shotgun into the side of the lookout's head, as I came in fast through the swinging doors with my lever action shotgun up and sweeping the room. "Sheriff's department—this is an arrest!" I yelled.

The lookout tumbled down the stairs as Bob leaned over the railing, pointing his shotgun down at a table. I noticed there was now complete silence in the room. My view was partly obscured by a woman, but I saw the Thorndyke boys, Henry and Harvey, sitting at a table with a big red haired man and two others. They all started to stand up, reaching for their guns.

"Throw your hands up!" Bob yelled.

Everyone was either trying to look up at Bob, or look over at me, or maybe Wes, all at the same time.

I focused my aim on Henry Thorndyke's fancy vest.

Out of the corner of my eye I saw some movement over at the end of the bar. I turned my head just in time to see Wes draw and fire his .45.

A women screamed. That sound was lost in the sound of gunfire.

Half a dozen guns were all firing at once.

I turned my head back to see all the men at that table pulling their own guns, some had already drawn. Bob and I fired at the same time. I saw the muzzle flashes and stabs of flame from a couple of other places in the room. Henry Thorndyke took my first shot in the side of his chest, and his gun went flying toward the ceiling. My second shot turned another man's head into stew meat. He was firing at me just as his head came apart.

Bob unloaded both barrels into Harvey Thorndyke from about five feet above him. The black powder smoke was obscuring my vision and I found myself moving to my right, toward the bar. I saw a man on my left with a gun pointed at me, and I shot him as he fired. My shot caught him in the crotch, and knocked his legs out from under him, slamming him face first into the floor. I was levering a new shell into the chamber, but I slipped and lost my balance. I saw the big red-headed man firing at me, but as I swung toward him, my shotgun snagged on an overturned table leg. I dropped it and dived for the floor, pulling my .45. There was a continual roar of gunfire.

Then silence.

34.

I found myself half kneeling, as I fed new shells into my .45.

I became aware of crying, whimpering, and an occasional groan. I could sort of see Bob still standing on the stairs, with his .45 in one hand, and a pocket pistol in the other.

The room was filled with a bluish haze of gun smoke. Tables and chairs lay turned over in pools of blood mixed with liquor, from the spilled bottles and drinks. Everyone in the room was down on the floor, except for Wes who still stood with his feet wide apart.

He was holstering his gun. He missed the holster the first time he tried.

For a moment I thought all of those people on the floor in the room had been shot. Some of them had been, but most of them had simply tried to get down out of the line of fire.

People began to get up slowly and carefully. At first, only one or two at a time got up, keeping their hands where we could see them. Most of the women were crying, but one was clearly in shock and unable to speak or focus her eyes. A friend helped her up and led her out of the building through the front door.

Then there was a sudden mass rush for the doors, and I let them all go.

I noticed a trail of blood spatters left behind. Evidently some of them were wounded. I figured most likely some, or all of the wounded, had been shooting at me a moment or so ago.

I discovered the reason I was half kneeling was because I'd been shot through the outside of my right calf. It was bleeding profusely. I must've slipped on the blood. There was also a burning sensation at the base of my neck where it joined the shoulder on the left side. I was bleeding there, too.

Wes walked over to a man who was down, but leaning against the bar. A quick head count told me there were eight men down, in all.

Bob started down the stairs. He helped the lookout man up to his feet and after pulling the man's revolver from the holster, he pushed him toward the door.

Now, only seven men down. Two of them were Thorndykes. I had no idea who the other five dead men were. An unknown number had been wounded.

I limped over to where Wes had kneeled down next to the man leaning against the bar. Bob joined us. I recognized the man now. He looked different, with different clothes, and he had shaved off his beard, but I knew him.

"Howdy, Wes. Never thought you could beat me," the man said weakly. He was shot to pieces.

"Howdy, Andrew, I'm sure sorry I had to. You shouldn't have gone for your gun. I was some surprised to see you here."

"Small world," Andrew mumbled. He was fading.

"Andrew, I'm afraid I've killed you—are you sure you're going to heaven?" Wes asked him.

Bob gave Wes a startled look.

"Hell, I fear is where I'm headed. Always was, Wes. I guess you know that."

"Do you want to go to heaven, Andrew?"

"Oh yes, Wes. I do. I sure do, if it ain't too late."

Wes leaned down close to him and said some words the wounded man repeated.

"You'll soon be with Jesus, Andrew," Wes said.

"Oh! I swear, Wes, I think I see Him . . . ."

The man died.

***

After a moment, I spoke up. "Wes, I heard you call him Andrew, but this man was Tom Russel," I said.

"Maybe that was the name he was using, but he was known all over Kansas, Missouri, Minnesota, and the Dakotas, as Andy 'Point Blank' Peterson.

For the last few years he's been traveling with a man by the name of Snooker Watson. They were bad outlaws. Watson didn't start off bad, but he threw in with Andrew here, and it ruined him. I don't know where Watson is but if Andrew is here, Watson is somewhere close by."

I shook my head.

"No, Watson was killed by my deputy Charlie Owens. I've heard of 'Point Blank' Peterson. I have paper on him in my office. The reward from Wells Fargo alone is five thousand dollars. How did you know him?"

"He was my half-brother. He killed my father, and ran off to fight in the war. He never stopped robbing and killing after that."

"He was wanted all over the country," I observed.

"Not anymore," Wes said, as he tried to stand.

And then Wes collapsed to the floor. A quick examination showed he'd been shot in the right shoulder and he was bleeding badly. The wound had been hidden from sight under his slicker. He'd fainted from trauma and loss of blood.

"Here, I'll take care of Wes. You need to take care of yourself, John. You've been shot too, you know," Bob said.

I realized my shirt was sticking to me and my right boot was filled with blood. I pulled my tie off and used the tie as a bandage around my calf. I reached up and felt the wound at the base of my neck. It wasn't too bad, just a flesh wound, but it had bled enough to stain my nice white shirt almost completely red. It probably looked worse than it was.

There was movement at the door.

Bob and I both had our guns on Sheriff Tommy Turner as he walked into the room with his hands held high.

"Don't shoot me, please don't shoot. I've come to help," Tommy said.

"Too late, get a mop." Bob said.

"Yeah, you've made a hell of a mess," Tommy observed.

"Tommy, go get a doctor!" I spat.

"We ain't got one. The nearest thing to a doctor we had was the bartender here, but I see you've killed him, too."

I knew I hadn't. I looked at Bob, who shook his head. He hadn't shot the bartender either. It must've been Wes or a loose shot fired by someone else. I looked at the man as he lay sprawled on the floor at the end of the bar. He had a sawed off double-barreled shotgun in his left hand.

"It was me. I shot that man," Wes groaned. He was awake again.

"Damned good thing you did—if he had opened up on us with that thing, one or more of us would be dead for sure," Bob said.

Wes shook his head weakly.

"Tommy, we need some help in here. Where can we get help for the wounded?" I asked.

"There's a woman over at Aphrodite's Bower. She was a nurse in the war. I hear she's pretty good with wounds," Tommy said.

"Well, go fetch her, NOW!" I yelled.

He took off at a run.

I looked at my watch.

It was just now eight forty five.

***

Shortly later, Mrs. Poole and Nancy came bustling into the building in the company of Max.

"Wes, I hear you've managed to get yourself shot again!" Mrs. Poole exclaimed. "Nancy, please have a look at him, while I see to the Sheriff here."

She looked first at my neck wound and indicated it wasn't serious but needed cleaning. She'd just begun to undo the makeshift bandage on my leg when Nancy interrupted.

"We need to get Mr. Spradlin to the house quickly, Emma. He needs more help than I can give him here. He has a bullet in him that has to come out."

"Ah'll take him, Miz Emma," Max volunteered.

"Thank you, Max. Please hurry," Mrs. Poole said.

Max scooped Wes up off the floor and cradled him in his arms like a baby. He and Nancy hurried out the door.

Mrs. Poole surveyed the room looking for other injured people. She confirmed everyone still on the floor was indeed dead. She asked Bob if he was hurt. He just shook his head.

"I don't know how even one of you could have survived this," she said sadly.

"I never wanted it to go this way. I intended to make an arrest of just two people, and it turned into a blood bath," I said.

"Well, all I can say is when you say you're going to clean up a town, you manage to take out most of the trash yourself."

"Not like this. Why did everybody start shooting?" I asked.

"I guess there were several men in here who didn't want to be arrested this evening. You killed Martin Pogue. He was sitting at the table with the Thorndykes.

He couldn't afford to be arrested. He faced hanging for sure. He just lost his head," Bob said.

"This place was a den of low life criminals, cutthroats, and thieves. A pity you didn't get Ian McGregger while you were at it. Can you walk, Sheriff?" Mrs. Poole asked me.

I nodded.

"I can hobble pretty well."

"Bob, you'd better help him up. We're going to the house to get you all patched up."

"Okay, Emma," Bob replied

It dawned on me they knew each other.

"How do you two know each other?" I asked, stupidly.

They both just stared at me.

I limped over and picked up my John Browning designed Winchester shotgun from where I'd dropped it. I reloaded it with shells from my jacket pocket.

Then we headed out.

***

Outside, the street was crowded with onlookers and some who had escaped the carnage. People had come running as soon as the shooting stopped. Some were standing on the porch of the Gold Dust. Others had swarmed out of the Oxbow.

There were horrified looks on the faces of some. Others nodded their respects.

There was no sign of Homer Thorndyke.

Bob and I were in no mood for trouble, and people could sense it. They moved aside and let us be on our way. I managed to limp around the corner, but before we had gone very far, I had to lean on Bob. Mrs. Poole hurried on ahead of us.

35.

Upon our arrival at Aphrodite's Bower, Bob eased me down on the couch in the music room.

Wes was nowhere in sight.

Victoria came in with a big bowl of hot water, bandages, towels, and what not.

She took one look at me and said, "Let's get your pants off. In fact, we need to get you out of your clothes altogether."

She looked at Bob, who had a peculiar grin on his face.

"You help him do that while I go upstairs and get a blanket," She said.

The minute she left the room, Bob chuckled.

"I would love to see the look on your face when you tell Lora this part of the story."

Before I could reply, Max came in.

"Y'all's friend is upstairs with Miz Emma, Nancy, and Debbie. He's hurt real bad."

I didn't like the sound of that.

"Bob, please go up and check on him. Maybe we should haul him down to Bear Creek, and let Doc Johnson treat him."

Bob nodded and left.

"Max, can you help me get my boots off?"

"Sho nuff, Sheriff Sage, you sit down there, and I'll ease um off."

The first one, on the left side, came off easy enough, but the one on the right was much more difficult. The bullet had gone through part of the calf muscle just above the top of my boot. That boot was full of sticky congealed blood. Max got a firm grip on the boot, and I grabbed my leg just above the knee and pulled my foot free. The effort was rewarded with tremendous pain and new bleeding from both my leg and the base of my neck. I lay back on the settee panting and sweating.

"Oh, for crying out loud! Men! You haven't got the sense God gave a chipmunk. Look at the mess you're making," Victoria said, as she hurried back into the room. "Here now, Sheriff, stand up for a minute. I swear men can't tolerate even a little pain."

Max helped me up, and I stood on one leg while Victoria draped the blanket over the couch. My blood saturated sock was steadily dripping onto the polished oak of the floor. "Max, put a towel under that foot!" Victoria snapped.

Max hastened to comply.

"Alright now, let's get you out of those clothes. We'll start with the slicker, then the gun belt, the jacket, vest, and shirt."

She helped me do that, then she had me peel down the top of my long johns to the waist. The long johns were stiffening with dried blood. Then she had me unbutton my pants and sit on the couch. She used some soap and warm water to bathe the bullet crease at the base of my neck and wash the blood off of my torso.

"Just hold this bandage on here for a little while, till the bleeding stops," she said.

Bob came back into the room.

"Wes can't be moved, till the bullet comes out. She's doing that now. I don't know of any doctor anywhere could do a better job than she's doing right now. She has her own surgical kit. You can tell she has done all this before."

"She has indeed," Victoria agreed. "In the war, Nancy treated simple bullet wounds and sewed up sabre cuts and bayonet wounds while the doctors handled the more complicated surgeries and amputations. She saw more wounded men on any given day than most fancy hospitals see in a year,"

"The war ended more than twenty years ago. She can't be that old," I said.

"Well, I don't know how old you think she is, but she was only a teenage girl when she worked in the field hospitals."

Victoria untied my tie and un-wrapped it from around my calf where it had functioned as a makeshift bandage.

"Max, he won't be needing this anymore. We'll have to throw away his shirt as well; even Ophelia couldn't get the blood stains out of that," she sniffed. "Now stand up. You can wrap this towel around your waist while you peel out of your pants, socks, and that union suit. We'll be able to wash the pants, socks, and underwear, and we'll sew up what holes we can."

I did as she said, observing the wound in my calf was bleeding less now. She bathed the wound and washed the blood off the rest of my leg and foot. We could see the bullet wound clearly now. The entry wound was an angry, puckered hole, but the exit wound was torn and nearly twice the size of the entry wound.

"That's going to leave a scar," she observed. "I see you have a few others already. I'll bind it up, but Nancy will want to have a look at it. She may want to throw a few stiches in there."

When she started bandaging it, she sent Max away with my clothes to be washed.

Mrs. Peele came into the room, looking drawn and pale.

"Bob, I believe the sheriff needs a drink. I know I do. Would you be so kind as to go grab some glasses and a bottle from the kitchen? Thank you."

She looked at me sitting on the couch with nothing on but a towel wrapped around my waist. She walked over and drew the blanket up around me, somewhat absent mindedly.

"Lay back sheriff," Victoria said. "You'll need to keep that leg propped up on this cushion."

I was worried about Wes.

Mrs. Poole filled me in.

"Nancy got the bullet out of Wes' shoulder. He lost a lot of blood in the process. He's weak as a kitten, but Nancy says he'll recover. He may have some loss of function in his right arm. He shouldn't be moved for a few days. I shall have to delay our move from here until maybe this weekend."

I nodded. I was feeling very, very tired.

When Nancy came in, I could see she was mighty tired as well.

"Let's have a look at your leg. You can stop holding the bandage on your neck, Sheriff," she said.

I took it away, seeing it was only slightly stained with blood.

Nancy looked at the neck wound and nodded confirmation that it wasn't serious.

"I think it will do fine without a bandage. It'll heal quickly. You will need to keep it clean though."

Bob came in with a bottle and several glasses. He started pouring whisky.

She took the bandage off my leg.

"Hmmmm, I don't think I should put any stiches in this. It will need to drain."

She reached out for a glass of whisky and poured some of it into the wound. I yelped, and she laughed. She tossed back the rest of the whiskey.

"Let's keep it bandaged with clean bandages. Change them at least once a day. You can have Doc Johnson keep an eye on it down in Bear Creek. Try not to walk far or put much weight on it for a few days. You'll know how much is too much. It'll be safe to walk on it a little, starting tomorrow. If it feels like it's tearing or starts to bleed a lot, get off it and use crutches."

She put a fresh bandage on it and bound it up firmly.

Debbie distributed the drinks, and Mrs. Poole raised her glass in a toast.

"To life," she said.

We clinked glasses together all around.

After a couple of stiff shots of whiskey, I started to nod off. "Let's clear out of this room and let the Sheriff get some rest," Mrs. Poole said.

I was too tired to discuss the options, so as soon as they were gone I fell into a deep sleep.

That sleep was tormented by horrible dreams augmented by the pain in my leg. I kept re-living the shootout and seeing men die. The woman with the blank expression floated before me. She asked me several times, "*Why?*" then her head flew apart.

***

I awoke at first light chilled and with a horrible taste in my mouth. I lay there for a while until I became aware of the smell of coffee and cooking bacon.

Bob came into the room carrying my clothes.

"Nancy will be along shortly to put a fresh bandage on your leg. Then you can get dressed.

Ophelia sends her best.

These are still a bit damp, but nearly dry. The ladies even found you a shirt. It was left here by some fella who had to take off in a hurry. It seems he did something to offend one of the ladies, so Max threw him out. Poor man landed in the yard wearing nothing but is under drawers. I'm pretty sure the shirt will fit.

The boots might be too big, but we didn't think to clean the blood out of yours last night."

"Uuuuh, thanks," I managed.

"Whenever you get dressed, come on into the dining room, and indulge in the fine breakfast Ophelia has prepared for us."

"Bob, we're going to have to get Tommy to help us identify some of those bodies."

"I have already addressed the issue and you may be assured Sheriff Tommy Turner will have affidavits ready for us later this morning. I went back out last night and took care of our horses. After breakfast, I'll go to the livery stable, get the horse harnessed and bring Wes' buggy over here, so you'll be able to drive it back down to Bear Creek, after we visit with Tommy."

"Well, aren't you 'Johnny on the spot'? What motivated you to get out early and build a fire under Tommy?"

Before he could answer, Nancy came in with hot water and fresh bandage material.

"I'll leave you to Nancy's gentle administration. Get dressed and come along to breakfast."

"Bob, I asked you a question."

"Right, so you did. We'll discuss it at length in due course. At this juncture I find myself in need of coffee and vital sustenance. Come along when you can."

He nodded and left.

I groaned.

Bob was back to his usual tricks.

"Does it hurt that much?" Nancy asked, concerned.

"Not, my leg, Nancy—it's attempting constructive conversation with Bob. It always hurts a lot."

"Really? That's odd, I find him quite charming."

I had to laugh.

***

I was pleased to discover that whoever had done my laundry had done a fine job. They'd even sewed up the bullet holes. There were two additional holes in my slicker though, where bullets had come close. When I went to put on my gun belt, I discovered the source of the big bruise that had come up on my left hip. A bullet had passed between the holster and the belt, taking a chunk out of the belt. I hadn't noticed it when I took the gun belt off.

"Now then, I want to know what it is you're up to Bob," I said, as I limped into the dining room.

Everyone was seated around the table except Mrs. Poole and Wes, of course.

"Well I must say, John, it's quite rude of you to ignore these ladies and fail to offer so much as a 'thank you' or even 'good morning,'" Bob replied haughtily.

I ground my teeth. He was right, I had forgotten my manners.

"Ladies, please forgive me. Thank you very much for all you've done for us, myself in particular," I said, with a slight bow from the waist.

"Think nothing of it Sheriff. I understand. You haven't even had any coffee yet this mornin'. My man is the same way," Ophelia said, as she poured me a cup of coffee.

"You might as well poke a bear with a stick as bother a man before he's had his coffee," she concluded.

"Yes ma'am. However, not an excuse, please do excuse my manners."

"John, perhaps our conversation can wait until we get the chance to include Wes in our deliberations. I think that would be the most propitious time." Bob said.

Nancy had told me she thought Wes would be able to talk to me after breakfast.

"Fine Bob, we'll do it then, right after breakfast."

***

After a breakfast of bacon and biscuits with honey and about a half pot of coffee in me, I was ready to brave an attempt at going up the stairs.

"If you use only your left leg to lift yourself, one step at a time, you'll save yourself considerable pain and avoid opening the wound again," Nancy said. "You can sort of hop down the stairs."

"Good advice, thank you."

We found Wes propped up in a sitting position in a bed in the first bedroom on the right, at the top of the stairs. Mrs. Poole was sitting in a chair doing needlepoint. Wes wore no shirt, but he was heavily bandaged and looked quite pale. He managed a weak smile when he saw us.

"John, I'm glad you're okay. Bob and I've come to an agreement and I want to hear your thoughts," he said.

Bob picked up the narrative.

"John, I talked to Wes about this earlier this morning. I'm going to collect the reward on Andrew Peterson and two of the other men. I won't try to collect on the Thorndyke boys, as apprehending them was the reason you came up here."

"No, Bob, we talked about this. You're a Deputy Sheriff of Alta Vista County. You can't claim any reward money for anybody you arrest or kill in the course of your duty."

"John, apparently it hasn't occurred to you that you failed to swear in Wes here as a deputy. He's a civilian.

Further you are clearly unaware of my actual status at the time. You see, I left a letter addressed to you in the care of Chief Deputy Charlie Owens. It was a letter of resignation, John, effective immediately as of yesterday's date, at noon.

I was not a deputy last night. Therefore, I can in fact collect reward money on anyone I apprehended or killed in the course of my duties as a bounty hunter."

I couldn't believe what I was hearing.

This was all wrong.

"Wes, are you willing to let him collect reward money on your own brother?"

"John, Andrew was my half-brother, same mother but different fathers. Andrew and my father never got along. When he killed my dad, I swore if I ever saw him again I'd kill him. He intended to kill me first, for the last twenty five years. I changed, but he didn't. I want something good to come from his death."

"Forget it! I was in pursuit of him as well, for his part in the bank robbery. Although I thought he was a man named Tom Russel. I don't see anything good coming from Bob collecting reward money for his death!"

"John, calm down. I don't need all this excitement," Wes said. "Besides, there's something you don't know."

I was still struggling with the whole ridiculous situation.

"Yeah, what else is new? This is surely the morning for surprises."

"Bob is collecting the reward money for me." Wes said.

"What? You're going to collect the reward money—I don't understand."

"John, Bob is collecting the reward money so I will have enough money to build a church and maybe start a school, here in North Fork."

I couldn't really wrap my mind around that.

I had something else I needed to do.

"Mrs. Poole, Bob, I have to ask you to step out of the room for a moment. Wes and I have something to discuss," I said. "Bob, please go get the buggy and bring it back over here."

Mrs. Poole looked at Wes, who nodded solemnly.

Bob held the door for her as they walked out.

When the door was closed behind them, I looked at Wes.

"Wes, I'm sorry but this is the end for you."

"How's that—what do you mean?" he asked.
"I've come up here to kill you."

36.

Wes narrowed his eyes at me.

"I'm not quite myself this morning, John, would you repeat that?"

"I said, you're finished, your days are done, and I'm here to kill you."

I watched him look quickly around to where his gun belt was hanging on a bedpost. It was behind and above him on his right side. It might as well have been in a different room. He knew he'd never be able to reach it before I shot him. He looked back at me. "Why?" he asked, sadly.

"Wes Spradlin, the gunman, showed up in a saloon in North Fork last night. He killed two men in a gun battle."

Wes nodded.

"...And?"

"And as long as he lives someone will be looking to take him in a gun fight.

It's time for Wes Spradlin to die and disappear into history and legend. It's time for a new preacher to appear in North Fork. Maybe a man named Les Bradley, or Jeff Sandlin, or whatever name you want to use. Plenty of people saw the shoot out where Wes Spradlin was shot down and killed. Today, the old man dies for good and a new man will emerge from the ashes."

Wes' eyes were shining.

"Do you really think it could work?" he asked.

I shrugged.

"You'll never get a better chance than this."

"What about all the witnesses and the people here?"

"Aside from Bob and me, there are only six people in this town who know you're still alive. Every one of them is in this house. Mrs. Poole will keep your secret and I imagine she can get the others to agree to the plan as well. Other than Ophelia, everyone will be moving on to Denver, where they can spread the word that Wes Spradlin died after being shot in a saloon up at North Fork."

Maybe Wes was crying, or maybe his eyes were just watering from all the gun smoke of the previous evening.

"Adios, Wes," I said.

I turned to leave the room.

"Wait, John," he said. "Do you see it? The old man is dead to sin and the new man is born again. I had no idea how I could put the old life behind me and really get on with my new life in Christ. I was carrying too much baggage and too many people wanted to see me fall. This is a chance, John, a real chance. How can I ever thank you?"

I shrugged. "You took up the gun again to help me. I expect I would be dead if you hadn't. I feel pretty bad about it. So, please, Wes, don't thank me. Thank God."

I stepped out of the room and pulled the door closed.

***

I found Mrs. Poole waiting for me down in the foyer.

"Mrs. Poole, the man upstairs has some things he wants to talk to you about. He has some interesting news. Please accept my apologies for complicating your life in this way. I can't thank you enough for your kindness and generous hospitality…"

She interrupted, holding up a hand.

"Sheriff, the 'Man Upstairs' has been trying to talk to me for years. Here lately, I've been listening to Him more than ever before."

She smiled.

"Yes, ma'am, I take your meaning. Anyway, speaking personally and on behalf of the Sheriff's department, I thank you very much. Bob and I will be leaving now. You let me know if you need any help with anything in the next few days, or with the move."

She walked over and retrieved my hat from the coat rack.

"Oh my, Sheriff, I'm afraid there is a bullet hole in this as well."

She held it up so I could see the hole through the brim.

"That was nearly a new hat," I grumbled. "Oh well, better the hat than the head. I guess."

"Indeed, much better. Please be careful, Sheriff," she said, by way of farewell.

I limped outside and stood on the porch for a moment.

It was a beautiful, high-mountain morning with just a hint of autumn's crispness in it. Though it was August and still summertime, at this altitude autumn was already beginning in North Fork. The Aspen leaves were starting to yellow. Soon they would be golden, and shortly later the snow would fall.

I saw Bob coming along the lane with the buggy. I noticed his horse wasn't tied behind it.

***

Bob and I walked into the Jubilee House looking for Sheriff Tommy Turner.

"He's in his office," the bartender said, pointing to the door near the back of the building.

We found Tommy sitting at the round table in his office. He was finishing the affidavit of facts and listing the names of those killed in the gun battle the night before. He was just finishing the list of those killed or wounded in the shooting.

"Good morning, Sheriff Sage. You're looking none the worse for wear this morning."

He nodded at Bob, by way of greeting.

"I'm just finishing this up."

"Tommy, let me see the affidavit before you sign it."

"Well sure, here you go," he said, spinning it around on the table top.

"You know, you were damn lucky everyone you killed last night had either been wanted or had fired on you; both I guess. There could've been innocent bystanders killed. You'll read in there where I mentioned some of the innocents were wounded."

"Tommy, there wasn't anybody in that saloon who could have been called an 'Innocent,'" Bob said.

"Maybe, but I meant people who were not involved in the shooting,"

"You mention here that Ian McGregger was seriously injured." I said.

"Yeah, well, he was. He was shot in the hand. Lost his pointer finger and his right hand is pretty badly mutilated."

"He was shooting at me at the time," I said.

"He claims he wasn't."

"He was."

"That is correct. Indeed, I saw him fire a number of shots. I would have disposed of the man myself, but I was otherwise occupied at the time," Bob said.

Tommy shrugged

"He says he wasn't."

"There's another thing you failed to mention here," I said, tapping the paper.

"Yeah, what's that?"

"Wes Spradlin died as a result of wounds he received in the gun battle."

I saw Bob give a little involuntary jerk. He glanced at me with some evident approval.

"Oh, I didn't know for sure. I saw that big black feller carry him off to Aphrodite's Bower. He died, huh?"

I nodded, sadly.

"Oh sorry, was Spradlin a friend of yours?"

I shrugged.

"We just met recently. One of the single most dangerous men I've ever met. It wouldn't be good to be on the wrong side of Wes Spradlin. But, he was shot down by 'Point Blank' Peterson, you know."

I watched Tommy's face light up.

"Now that *is* something. Two top guns, killed right here in North Fork—how about that?"

"It's not something to be proud of, Tommy."

"Maybe not, but it will put us on the map for a while. Just think of it, 'Point Blank' Peterson and Wes Spradlin killing each other in a shootout. People will talk about it for years!"

I shrugged, again.

"Don't you think you'd better write it into the affidavit?"

"Yep, I'm on it," he said, spinning the paper back around. He scribbled away for a while.

"Don't forget to mention that McGregger fired on peace officers in his saloon," Bob said.

"He says he didn't."

"Tommy, you have called me a liar for the last time." Bob said, coldly.

Tommy froze, is eyes as big as saucers.

"Oh, uh, well, no I, uh, it's just that, uh—I have conflicting stories."

"No, you do not. Write it down, now.

Tommy looked at me.

"I'll tell you how this is going to work, Tommy," I began. "When you finish writing, we'll walk over to the post office and get this Affidavit and Statement of Facts witnessed by the Post Master and one other person, while you sign it. Then, you're going to make a big sign which says 'CLOSED BY ORDER OF THE COUNTY SHERIFF,' and you're going to nail it up on the Gold Dust Hotel and Casino.

If there are any employees or guests still on the premises, they are to be evicted. I'm sending a deputy sheriff up here tonight or tomorrow to make sure you did it. If not, he will arrest you for obstruction of justice and drag you back to Bear Creek in irons. Then I will come up here with a posse and burn your place to the ground, along with the Gold Dust, and we'll tear down the Oxbow in the process. I'll be back here and you'll be in jail and out of business. Do you have any questions or comments?"

"Well, what about Ian McGregger? He won't like it. He'll be mad as hell in fact."

I shook my head. I thought Tommy had more sense.

"Where is he? We'll take it up with him, right now." I said.

"I heard someone took him down to Bear Creek last night, to get his hand doctored."

I slapped the top of the table.

"Okay, then, you won't have a problem with him today. Stand up and start acting like a lawman. As long as I have your cooperation, I will stand by the terms of our agreement. You have the rest of the thirty days to get this town in order. I expect we've given you a pretty good head start."

He thought about it for a moment.

"Yeah, all right I can do that," he nodded.

"You can, and you will, or you won't believe what happens to you and this town in the next twenty four hours,"

He looked some put out.

"Okay, I said I'll do it."

"Good decision, now finish writing this affidavit."

***

After the affidavit was signed by Tommy, me, and two witnesses, we walked back over to the Jubilee House.

"Well, Tommy, I hope I won't have occasion to see you again anytime soon."

"Yeah, me too," he agreed.

"You'll be meeting my deputy, like I said, tonight or tomorrow."

"Yeah, I can hardly wait," he growled.

"And, there's another fella you'll be meeting soon. There's a preacher coming here to start a church. I don't know his name, but I suspect he'll look familiar to you. I expect you to give him your full support. There'd better not be one bit of trouble with him, or I'll hear about it."

"Shoot, that's no problem. Fact is there's been considerable talk about getting a church going up here. I'm not opposed to it at all," he said, brightly.

I grinned at him.

"That's good to know, Tommy, really good to know."

Bob was trying hard, and failing, to hide his smile.

Dan Arnold

37.

Bob's big black horse was tied at the hitching rail outside Tommy's Jubilee House. He walked over and got him, while I carefully climbed back into the buggy. He mounted the black and I slapped the reins on the back of the buggy horse. We started down the road for Bear Creek.

We rode along in silence for a few minutes, until Bob spoke up.

"That was an interesting turn of events. I admit, I never saw it coming. Don't get me wrong now. I held little hope there would not be gun play, although I knew you wanted to avoid it. Still the outcome of this little adventure has been, for lack of a better word, enlightening,"

I considered his choice of words.

"I'll admit I never anticipated you would have resigned your appointment as deputy sheriff."

"Ah, well, there is more than one way to skin a cat. I knew there would probably be an opportunity to reap some reward from the trip up here."

"I would've considered just finding and arresting the Thorndykes to be reward enough," I said.

Bob looked at me.

"Yes, you would. You see, that is the difference between us."

I chuckled.

"Well, Bob, it's one of them."

He nodded.

"The problem is you fail to grasp the simplicity of the Darwinian concept of survival of the fittest. You see, Mr. Darwin has explained there are inferior and superior strains in all aspects of biological life. The stronger prevail over the weaker. It's the natural order, my friend."

"I'm familiar with the theory."

"Well then, you must be aware criminals are by their very nature inferior humans and it follows that we being superior humans should prevail. In fact by removing the inferior criminal element we are improving the breed. It's rather the same principle as culling the herd."

I looked over at him.

"That is unmitigated horse shit, Bob."

He looked offended.

"In what way?"

"In several ways; the first is that human beings were created by God. We are not descended from apes, lizards, fish, or pond slime. I'm aware you don't believe it, but that's the way I see it..

Second; all people everywhere suffer from the same inferior imperfection. It's called sin, Bob. It is the way we are, naturally. You have it, I have it, and everyone everywhere has it. It's a fatal disease, and no one of us is superior to others; we are only different in the ways we manifest our sinful nature.

Third; the things we tend to think make someone superior—strength, height, speed, appearance, or even seeming intelligence—are relative as to whether or not they contribute to superiority and generally comparative within the context of a given time, place, and circumstance. What seems superior in one situation may be inferior in another.

For example, there are times and places when strength is inferior to speed, or speed is inferior to appearance, or appearance is inferior to intelligence, if you follow me.

Seldom does any individual have all of the attributes you might think are superior. Even those who do seem to have them are still flawed by their sinful nature.

Fourth; there is no proof people who commit crimes are somehow inferior human beings.

Fifth; the notion the strong have the natural right to eliminate the weak, for any reason whatsoever, is horribly wrong and a clear example of a different manifestation of the same exact sin nature I alluded to earlier. If a person thinks they are superior to someone else, they are morally flawed."

Bob smirked.

"Oh, well, my mistake. I might have expected you to be a bit backwards on this subject. You observe life through a religious lens. Science trumps religion every time though, John. Sorry, but it does."

I shook my head.

"Bob, you draw that word 'Science' as if you were drawing a gun. As if the mere use of the word 'Science' settled a matter. Remember what the word 'science' means. Science is the *study* of creation. Study, involves observation and experimentation, to form theories, not conclusions. Charles Darwin simply expounded a theory based on his personal observations. A *theory* is not a fact."

"Perhaps we should discuss something other than evolution." Bob suggested.

I grinned.

"I think you mean something other than the Darwinian theory of evolution."

He just frowned.

Bob gets frustrated, sometimes.

He changed the subject.

"Did you observe, as I did, a certain connection between Emma and Wes?"

I nodded in agreement.

"Well, they do have some history."

"Rather unseemly behavior for a preacher, don't you think?" Bob asked.

"I don't think so. Wes was a different man when he knew her in the past. They hadn't seen each other for more than a decade. I observed you have some familiarity with Mrs. Poole yourself."

Bob shrugged, in acceptance.

"Indeed, however our relationship has been purely professional."

"Hmmm, now how exactly do you mean that, Bob?"

He chuckled as he considered the implications.

"I first met Emma in Missouri, right after the war, when I was working as a Pinkerton agent. She was Emma Rafferty then, having not yet met Frank Poole. In her line of work, she was in a position to meet a variety of people without anyone paying much attention. She listened and learned things useful to me, and I was able to gather the information without drawing undue suspicion on either of us. It was a good business arrangement. She gathered intelligence on suspects for which I was willing to pay. We have continued that relationship on occasion over the years."

I nodded.

I'd suspected something of the kind.

"I suppose it was she who first gave you the tip on how to locate the Thorndykes," I said.

Bob gave me an innocent look.

"I never reveal my sources, John."

"Good policy," I observed.

We rode along in silence for a while.

"Bob, I have to say I'm pleasantly surprised by your generosity in collecting the reward money on Andrew Peterson, so Wes can build a church,"

He considered his response.

"I am not completely without character, John. I told Wes I intended to collect the reward on Martin Pogue, Zach Sherman, and Smiley Burnett. I didn't know for sure whether Sherman and Burnett were among the dead until I talked to Tommy Turner this morning. Finding them in the saloon was exactly the sort of windfall I had hoped for. It's the reason I resigned from the sheriff's department.

Wes thought about it for a while, He was the one who pointed out the fact Peterson was wanted and Tom Russel was just a name he was using. Five thousand dollars is a lot of money. Wes indicated he couldn't collect the reward for personal reasons, but he wanted something good to come from the whole hideous affair. He suggested I should collect the reward for Peterson, as well as the others."

"It must've been tempting, didn't you think about just keeping the money?" I asked.

Bob chuckled.

"Oh, yes. Five thousand dollars is nearly five years of salary, if I'm working for you. At first I was quite tempted, but considering Pogue, Sherman, and Burnett together will bring me that much, I decided a fifty/fifty split would be more equitable."

I looked at him.

"Especially when you consider the fact Wes probably saved both of our lives, Bob,"

"Yes, I did consider that."

"How did you arrive at the idea of building a church?"

"I told Wes I wanted something good to come out of this as well. I asked him if he could think of a good use for the money."

"Well however you worked it out, I'm proud of you."

Bob was silent for a moment. Then he spoke up.

"I think I will come out ahead in this deal yet, John."

"Oh, in what way?"

"I plan to collect the reward on Homer Thorndyke as an added bonus. I'm free to do it now, and I expect the price on his head will go up."

I'd been thinking about Homer myself. Where was he? Why hadn't we found him in North Fork?

"Have you got any idea where to start looking for him?"

Bob shook his head.

"Not this morning, but I will pick up his trail in due course. I expect he won't run very far."

"Why is that?"

"Really, John, it's elementary. Have you no skill at recognizing the obvious. He won't go far because you are still alive. He'll want to kill you now, more than ever."

Dan Arnold

38.

As we approached the bridge over Bear Creek, my house on the edge of town came in to view. I could just barely see the kids playing in the yard.

"Bob, I have to stop at the house for a little while. Then, I need to go on into town. I want to talk to Doctor Johnson, and I need to get this affidavit recorded in the courthouse. I don't think I can make the walk back and forth. I'll need to use the buggy, but when I'm done with it, it has to go back to the parsonage."

"That is nothing to be concerned about. I shall be delighted to spend some time at your house. There is always the chance we can enjoy another late lunch, in the company of your lovely wife."

That's Bob, always thinking of the needs of others.

***

As I expected, Lora had been watching for me. She rushed out to meet us as we stopped at the gate. The delight was evident in her eyes.

"Darling, you're home! I've been so worried."

Bob was quicker to respond than I was.

"Why, thank you, Lora. I'm delighted to see you as well. You will note I brought your husband along with me. You do remember John, don't you?"

I was stepping carefully out of the carriage.

Lora ignored Bob's comment, but I shot him a look, as I swept her into my arms.

He grinned back at me, as he stepped down from his horse.

Lora looked into my eyes. "John, something has happened hasn't it? Where is Brother Spradlin?"

"Well, Baby, it's a long story. He stayed behind in North Fork. I'll tell you all about it when we get inside."

The kids were watching us through the fence.

"Well, howdy there!" I said, giving them a silly exaggerated wave and a goofy look. They both grinned and Sarah giggled.

I tried not to, but I found myself limping as we headed for the house.

"John, you're hurt!" Lora observed.

I nodded toward the kids. "It's nothing serious. I'll tell you about that too, in the house

She understood I didn't want the children hearing what had happened in North Fork.

She finally acknowledged Bob's presence.

"Bob, would you care to join us for lunch?"

"Well, if you insist. I would so hate to impose, although I am quite hungry as you will understand."

***

After lunch, the kids went back outside to play. It gave the adults a chance to talk.

I told Lora about the house inspection and then I told her about the gunfight.

I explained the story of Wes and his half-brother, Andrew Peterson, and how it ended in gunfire.

"Wes was wounded in the fight—now, don't worry he's going to be fine—but, Lora, I thought it would be a good opportunity for him to start a new life, with a new name. So, I have an affidavit swearing the notorious gunman, Wes Spradlin, was killed in the gunfight at the Gold Dust Saloon and Casino in North Fork, Colorado, last night."

Lora took a deep breath.

"Do you think it will really work?"

Bob butted in.

"The story will spread like wild fire. People who weren't even in North Fork last night will tell the tale of how they personally witnessed the shootout.

They'll tell stories about how Wes braced Peterson, or maybe it was the other way around. They'll tell the tale of how the two men stood in the middle of the bar and challenged each other. Each man slapped leather and no one could tell who was faster.

Did Wes Spradlin draw first or was it Peterson? There was the roar of gunfire and both men staggered and fell, shot through the heart with a single gunshot from the other man's gun, the two half-brothers standing face to face, and falling side by side at the end. The legend will grow with each telling, partly truth and partly myth."

"Why Bob, it sounds almost as if you were actually there," I observed.

"Well, I was there, wasn't I?"

"We both were. I pretty much wish I hadn't been there. Actually, I wish the whole thing hadn't gone the way it did."

"It isn't your fault, John. You didn't raise those Thorndyke boys. You didn't build the Gold Dust Saloon and make it a haven for the dregs of humanity. You didn't rob the bank, and kill a man in the process. It's part of the work you've chosen to do, but it isn't your fault it happened the way it did," Bob stated. "No one could have predicted there would be several men in that saloon who would rather fight and die than be arrested."

I shrugged.

Lora said, "But what a horrible way to die, to be shot to death in a filthy saloon."

"Well, Lora, it could be argued those men met their demise in a place and manner of their own choosing. The evidence suggests they would have preferred that death to one by hanging in a public execution," Bob said.

I needed to bring some light to the discussion.

"Actually, how they died is not the point. Everyone dies. Whether we die by accident or illness, old age or incident, as children or adults, is unimportant. What is important is the way we choose to live the life we have, however long or short it may be. God will be the judge. I just wish I never had a part in sending them on to judgment."

"Again, John it is what you have chosen to do with the life you have. Is that not the life of a lawman, to bring suspected criminals to judgment?" Bob asked.

I sighed and nodded.

"That's part of it, though I prefer to make arrests and let a court of law determine their fate. Let a jury decide whether or not they're guilty. There's also the part about protecting the innocent and preventing crime in the first place," I said.

Bob acknowledged my comment with a slight nod of his head.

We all thought our own thoughts for a moment.

Lora knit her brows.

"Is it really right to use this kind of deception to give Brother Spradlin a new start?" She asked.

"I thought about it before I decided to give it a try. I decided the story hurts no one and it benefits everyone involved. Wes gets a new life with a new name. North Fork gets a new preacher and a new church. Alta Vista County and the city of Bear Creek won't have to deal with a bunch of gun fighters trying to make a reputation showing up and causing all manner of trouble. It's a win/win situation for everybody."

I don't know, John, it doesn't seem right—but then again, it just might work."

"Baby, I have to go into town for a little while. Bob will drive me home as soon as I take care of a couple of things I must do. I'll be back as quick as I can," I said.

"That's fine, honey. As long as I know you're okay, and you'll be home soon, all is right with the world," Lora said.

I wrapped her up and kissed her.

"I guess we'll be in need of another pastor now. I wonder if Bud and Mildred will be able to return to Bear Creek. I'll write to them immediately," Lora mused.

***

Bob and I left her to her thoughts and plans and headed on into town.

Our first stop was at the courthouse. I had the affidavit recorded in the County Clerk's office. The clerk's eyes nearly bugged out when he read the details. I knew the story would be in circulation all over town within the day.

I found Chief Deputy Charlie Owens sitting behind my desk in the Sheriff's office. I could see Charlie was relieved to see us alive. We told him the story of why we had no prisoners.

Charlie looked at Bob.

"Well, Bob, do you still want me to give that letter to, John?" he asked.

"Indeed sir, if you would be so kind."

Charlie pulled a sealed envelope out of a desk drawer and handed it to me. I opened it and was not surprised to find it was exactly what Bob had told me it would be. He'd resigned, as of noon the previous day.

I sighed as I put the letter back into the envelope.

"Charlie, will you send Ed up here. I have an assignment for him."

"Yes sir, I'm on it."

When Charlie had gone, I offered to hand the letter back to Bob, but he shook his head.

I shrugged.

"We'll miss having you on the team, Bob. You're probably the best detective I know. I understand why the governor has confidence in your services,"

Bob smiled with real warmth.

"Thank you, John. I hope you understand this decision is purely based on my desire to pursue more lucrative economic opportunities, and in no way reflects on our friendship."

"I do, Bob."

"Further, I will be happy to offer my services at any time should you have need of me. In a private capacity of course, I find the constraints of uniform service unappealing."

"What are your plans?"

"As I indicated, I'm going to stay here in Bear Creek until Homer Thorndyke has been accounted for. Then, there is an opportunity down in New Mexico I might explore. I expect the governor will have an occasional assignment for me as well. The possibilities are endless for a man of my talents."

I nodded.

"I have no doubt."

"You should consider hanging up the badge and coming along with me. We could make a lot of money together."

I shook my head and smiled.

"Like I told you before, I know how that goes. You make good money, but it comes intermittently and at a high cost, and the way you like to live, it goes away pretty fast, too. The feast is followed by famine, and you just might get yourself killed somewhere in between. Besides, I prefer to represent the law. You feel no such obligation."

"True enough, although I have no real desire to operate outside the law, on occasion I may have to dance in the shadows, as it were. I have to apply my talents wherever the money is most readily available."

"Not for me, Bob."

He shrugged.

"Well then, 'to each his own,' as the saying goes, John."

Ed came in. I filled him in on the recent events in North Fork.

"I need you to go up there and make sure the Gold Dust is closed down and stays closed. Throw out anybody hanging around. You'll need to be tough. You can't count on Tommy Turner for anything. Be careful, be alert, and don't hesitate. You represent the law and you represent me. I'll back you no matter what you have to do; any questions?"

He took a moment to think about it.

"When do you want me to go?" He asked.

"How soon can you get your gear ready?"

"I'll leave within the hour."

I slapped him on the back.

"Okay, again, be careful and remember you won't have many friends up there."

He nodded, then he had another thought.

"One more question. How long do you want me to stay up there?"

"You come back anytime you need to. Otherwise, I want you to stay up there until the thirty days I gave them to clean up their act is up. It's just a couple of weeks, now. Make it stick, Ed."

"Yes sir. Adios then; I'm off to gather my things, and then I'll hit the trail."

"Oh, there's one more thing you should know."

I explained the story about the "death" of Wes Spradlin, and gave him some directions about handling the details of the burial of an empty coffin.

We shook hands and I clapped him on the back again, as he headed out the door.

"I have to go over and see Doc Johnson. I figure I can walk that far. Do you want to go with me?" I asked Bob.

"No, but when you get done over there, I'll be around here somewhere. I'll drive you back down to your house."

Dan Arnold

39.

I limped over to Doc Johnson's. He wasn't in his office, so I eased my way up the stairs to his rooms above his office. He answered my knock.

"John, how are you? I understand there was some serious shooting trouble up at North Fork, and you were in the middle of it. Is it over?"

"It is, Doc. How did you happen to hear about it?"

"I treated three men last night and this morning, all of whom were shot up. I gathered it must've been pretty horrific."

I nodded.

"Who did you treat and are they still here?"

"Two of them are downstairs in my office. A fellow named Murphy and a man named McGregger. They were brought down in a wagon last night. The third one left under his own power; Wilkins was his name. Why do you ask?"

"I'm looking for McGregger, how bad is he hurt?"

"He lost the index finger on his right hand and the bullet traveled through the rest of his hand and his wrist. I had to dig for the bullet and take some bone fragments out of his arm just above the wrist. I had to pretty much knock him out with laudanum to do the surgery. It's why he's still here. The hand is ruined. He may regain some use of it, but not much. I guess he's lucky, back during the war I would've had to amputate it."

"What about the other guy, Murphy?"

"Abdominal wound, the bullet went through, but I don't know..... If he lives through another night, he has a chance. He survived the wagon ride down out of the mountains, so he's pretty tough. We'll see. I was just headed down to check on them. Do you want to come with me?"

"I do."

"Just one thing, John . . . ."

I waited.

"No gun play, you understand? I think there's been more than enough of that."

I agreed completely.

"Is he armed?"

"No. There are no guns at all down stairs. I just don't need any more bullet wounds today, and neither do you."

"Actually, Doc, I wonder if you'd take a look at my leg. I got shot last night, too. The bullet went through a part of my calf."

"Good heavens, John, why didn't you say something sooner?"

When he saw the bandage he nodded with appreciation.

"It appears you've already seen a doctor somewhere."

"Sort of . . . ."

He examined the wound.

"This should heal well, John. Keep it firmly bandaged for a few more days. Change the dressing once a day and keep it dry. Come and see me if there's any new pain, if it gets red and angry looking, or if it starts bleeding."

He bandaged it up again with a fresh dressing and the same bandage.

***

I limped down the stairs ahead of him and then followed him into his office.

To one side of the office, at the back of the room, there was a screen around an examining area. Behind the examining area there was a door leading into a room with four beds. I'd been in the room before.

Today, two of the beds were occupied.

On one bed, a man fully dressed lay back against the pillows, his muddy boots on the bed. He had no gun I could see. His red hair and beefy body told me who he was. The heavily bandaged and splinted right arm and hand confirmed it. He was clearly groggy, but on seeing me, he became more alert.

The other man lay under bed covers across the room and appeared to be in a deep sleep, unaware of our presence.

I smiled as turned to the red haired man.

"Howdy, Mr. McGregger, I don't believe we've met. I'm the Sheriff, John Everett Sage is my name. I'd shake your hand but you seem to have a problem there. I hear somebody shot your trigger finger off."

I found pleasure in saying it.

He just looked sick.

Doc Johnson was checking the pulse on the other man. He felt the man's forehead and lifted an eyelid. Then he pulled back the covers to examine the bandages on the man's torso. He looked concerned about the results of his examination.

"I've had to give him a lot of laudanum. The pain was pretty much more than he could take. I was hoping he would be doing better than this by now,"

"How about Mr. McGregger here?"

Doc Johnson looked him over from the other side of the room.

"Mr. McGregger, you're good to go if you feel up to walking now. Come and see me in the morning and I'll change the bandage."

He looked at me.

"I guess I'm under arrest. Can you come to the jail?"

McGregger's speech was a bit slurred and he seemed disoriented.

I shook my head.

"No, that won't be necessary. You aren't under arrest. In fact, I'm going to let you leave town; I expect you to pull out of this county all together. And do it today."

He focused his gaze more fully on me.

"But all my money, everything I have is in a safe, in my saloon up at North Fork."

I shook my head again.

"Uh, uh. In about thirty minutes I'm going to put you on a stage headed east. You're done with North Fork. I closed down your saloon. You may recall the circumstances."

He was still a bit groggy, but he was getting the message.

"But, what about my money?"

I slapped him across the face.

"Your money should've been in a bank."

"Now, see here, Sheriff Sage. That was uncalled for," Doc Johnson began.

I cut him off.

"No, I need to have his full attention. This worthless piece of trash tried to kill me last night. He should've died in the fighting. Several other people did. He deserves to go to prison, but I won't spend the time or the resources holding him in my jail. I have to let him live and he gets to start over somewhere else, but I won't put up with his whining."

I turned my attention back to McGregger.

"You hear me, McGregger? You're done here, and you better run like a whipped dog."

McGregger's eyes had come into full focus now, and they were filled with hate for me.

"You're a dead man, Sage. I'll kill you for this," he said.

"You already tried that, 'Lefty.' Now, get up and I'll walk you over to the stage station."

40.

The stage to Ogallala, Nebraska was headed East with Ian McGregger on board. I knew he could get off at any stop and make his way back to North Fork, so I'd given him clear instructions not to try it. I made sure he understood he was not wanted anywhere in Alta Vista County and if he showed up, he would be treated the same way I would treat a rattler in the outhouse.

***

I was limping up Line Street back to the courthouse when Tom fell in beside me.

"I hear there was some shooting up in North Fork last night," he said.

I nodded.

"Yep"

"Is that why you're limping?"

"Uh huh."

I heard Wes Spradlin was killed. Is that true?"

We were right in front of the livery stable.

"Tom, I need to check on my horse. Have you got a minute to talk?"

"Sure."

We went through the barn, out to where Dusty was penned. I wished I had an apple or something to give him, but he seemed happy to see me anyway.

I'd chosen this spot because there were no ears to hear us, except Dusty's, and he never tells my secrets.

I told Tom the whole story.

"I've still got that wanna be gunfighter locked up in my jail. I can't wait to see the look on his face when I tell him Wes Spradlin was killed last night in a gunfight with "Point Blank" Peterson."

"Do you think he'll believe it?"

"I expect he will. When the story makes the papers, he'll believe it then."

""Now there's an idea. I believe I'll stop by the newspaper office and give Jerry Starnes a statement about the shooting."

"I'll go along with you. I want to see how he reacts."

***

We found publisher Starnes pounding away on a typewriter. He was proud of the fact he owned a typewriter and insisted on using it for all his correspondence with anyone and everyone.

"Gentlemen, how may I help you?" He asked.

"You know Mr. Starnes, when I was out in San Francisco; the Pacific Bell Telephone Company was stringing lines all over the city. I read your story in The Banner about how down in Denver there's quite a buzz going about telephone systems and how soon there will be a full telephone system in Denver. They say they already have one in Colorado Springs."

"I am well aware of that, Sheriff Sage, What's your point?"

"Oh, just that it's a real shame we don't have telephone lines between here and North Fork."

"And why is that, sir?"

"Well if we did, you would've already heard about the big gun fight up there last night."

"What, when did this happen? Hang on a minute."

He ripped out the page he had been typing on and wound a new sheet into the typewriter.

"Ok, now let's establish the facts. Who, what, where, when, and why this time, Sheriff? It seems wherever you go, there is going to be a shooting."

"That's an assumption on your part. I didn't say I was there."

"Were you there?"

I nodded.

"Are you ready to make a statement?"

I shrugged.

"I guess it's the only way I can get the truth into print."

Mr. Starnes frowned at that, but Tom was grinning.

"Last night, at about eight forty, I entered the Gold Dust Saloon and Casino in North Fork to make an arrest of the fugitives who had escaped from the County Jail on Saturday night."

He typed furiously for a minute or so, and then he held up his hand.

"Wait a moment. Were you alone?"

"I was the only lawman on the scene. Sheriff Tommy Turner refused to offer any assistance. Bob

Logan offered his assistance though, so no, I wasn't alone."

"Mr. Logan is a Sheriff's deputy."

"He was. He'd resigned his position prior to my going up to North Fork."

Starnes raised his eyebrows at the news. He dug out a stub of pencil and wrote something on the page he was typing on. He began typing away again. After a moment, he read over what he'd written so far.

"So, it would seem you and Mr. Logan entered the Gold Dust together."

Actually, I went in through the front doors and Bob came in through the back."

Mr. Starnes nodded and thought for a moment.

"OK, then what happened?"

"Upon entering the building I announced I was the Sheriff and I was there to make an arrest."

Starnes made a motion to urge me to continue.

"Well, there were several desperados in the building. There was "Point Blank" Peterson, Wes Spradlin, Martin Pogue, Zach Sherman and Smiley Burnett, among others."

"Hold on. Spell those names for me."

I spelled them out, one by one.

"Right, then what happened?"

"It seems Peterson and Spradlin had a long standing feud. They were half-brothers you know. Anyway, they squared off and one of them went for his gun and as soon as they moved, guns started coming out all around the room. It was just bad timing on my part. I had no idea I was going to walk into a gunfight."

Starnes typed furiously for a moment.

"Then what happened?"

"There was a great deal of gunfire. All of the gentlemen I listed were killed in the fighting, as were Henry and Harvey Thorndyke, the men I was hoping to arrest."

Mr Starnes stared at me with a shocked look on his face.

"Are you saying you and Bob Logan killed seven men in a gunfight?"

"I'm saying that when I attempted to arrest the fugitives, several men pulled guns and began firing on me and Bob. A gun fight ensued in which eight men lost their lives. I would point out six of those men were wanted, desperate and had a price on their heads."

"Eight, you only listed seven."

"Sorry, the bartender was killed as well. I didn't get his name. He attempted to shoot us with a sawed off shotgun. Wes Spradlin killed him. The thing between Peterson and Spradlin was what started all the shooting in the first place."

The newspaper man blinked several times, and then began typing again, more slowly this time. He stopped and read over what he'd written again.

"Let me see if I have this down correctly. You and Bob Logan walked into the Gold Dust last night to arrest the Thorndykes, and right when you walked in, Andrew Peterson and Wes Spradlin drew their guns and began shooting at each other. That prompted other men to draw their guns and fire at you. In the ensuing gun battle all of the outlaws were killed and you walked away without a scratch?"

"Well, actually I was wounded. Thank you for asking."

"Were there any witnesses to this gunfight?" Starnes asked, skeptically.

"Oh yes, at least twenty witnesses and there is an affidavit attesting to those facts filed of record in the courthouse."

"Sheriff, this is some story. I'll have to read the affidavit and interview some witnesses, but I'll have this out on the wire to every newspaper in the country. They eat this stuff up back east. My name will be published with the story wherever it gets printed!"

I hadn't thought it through. I never considered that other newspapers would pick up the story. I'd overlooked the obvious.

"I know for a fact, the governor asked you to clean up North Fork. Several people have told me you went up there and issued an ultimatum. The next thing we know, you walk into a saloon and a bunch of people get killed. This is sensational. You'll be the most famous lawman in the country; Wyatt Earp won't have anything on you."

"Now hold on a minute. I never intended to shoot anybody and it's a miracle Bob and I lived through it."

Where is Mr. Logan? I'll need to interview him as well," Starnes said, as he jumped up from behind his desk. He was still wearing his green visor.

"Bob is over at the courthouse."

Starnes grabbed a notepad and raced out of the building in his shirt sleeves with the sleeve garters on.

I felt bad about sending the newspaper man after Bob, but I needed a moment to think about what I'd done.

I looked over at Tom where he was seated in a chair by the door.

He just shook his head.

"I think you've put your foot in it now," he said.

"I know, Tom. This is what I get for trying to be clever. Another thing...you were right. It was a foolish notion Bob and I could arrest the Thorndykes in North Fork without any shooting. You told me, but I underestimated the consequences. I felt like I needed to get the situation under control and I rushed into it. The whole thing has blown up in my face and people are dead because of me."

He was thoughtful for a moment.

"In the whole big scheme of things, John, I believe you are being a little hard on yourself. You've done the county a service. Bob told me he was watching your house because the Thorndykes meant to kill you the first chance they got. You are a bit headstrong. It's just not in your nature to wait or try to figure out the safest way to do something. But, it's over now and we'll just move on from here."

I wished he was right, but I knew better.

"But it's not over, Homer Thorndyke is still out there somewhere. Every sensation seeker in the country is going to want to come to Bear Creek and North Fork to see me and see where the shootout happened. I wanted to help Wes disappear and start a new life in an obscure corner of the world. Now he'll have to go somewhere else or hide out till the storm blows over."

41.

By the middle of the afternoon I'd done all I could do. Tom and I found Bob strolling down the street with Lacey Courtney on his arm. Bob seemed quite pleased with himself. No doubt the newspaper interview had given him opportunity to be a big man in Lacey's eyes.

Lacey was in town to do some shopping. She was dressed in a sky blue outfit, a matching jacket and skirt with a nautical theme, sort of like a sailor's uniform. She even had a stylized sailor's cap with long blue ribbons hanging down the back. The outfit was stylish and frivolous all at the same time. Perfect for Lacey. It reminded me of how immature she really was.

***

On the ride down to the house I opened up the subject of Bob's relationship with Lacey.

"Are your intentions toward her entirely honorable, Bob?"

He grinned and gave me a wink.

"Well no, perhaps my intentions could not be characterized as entirely honorable. After all she is a high-spirited filly and she is ready to be broken in."

"Bob, I'm going to pretend you did not just say that."

"Oh, now, don't take on so. I know you don't approve of my attitude. I'm merely observing a natural fact. I have no intention of doing anything inappropriate."

"I'm glad to hear it. She's practically engaged to Glen Corbett."

"Everyone seems to think so, but the young lady in question is in fact quite available."

"She'll make a fine wife for someone, Bob, but if you'll pardon my saying so—you ain't the man."

"Oh, I don't know about that. She is beautiful and wealthy. Her family owns the largest ranch in the county. I could see myself ensconced as lord of the manner."

I snorted at that.

"What, you don't think I could settle down and become a part of the landed gentry?"

"Bob, you never stay in any one place for very long. You spend more money than you make, and you are very fond of charming your way into the hearts and the pant. . . uh. My point is you love the ladies, Bob."

He nodded.

"All too true I fear."

"You would also have a very hard time trying to win over her father. As you are no doubt aware, Bill Courtney is no fool. He's hoping Lacey will marry Glen Corbett. If you were to marry Lacey, I expect Bill Courtney would cut you off and her right along with you.

Glen is the kind of man who sticks through thick and thin. He's a builder, Bob. The kind of man a woman needs. Glen is as solid as a rock. You, my friend, are more like a tumbleweed.

"Ah, you've wounded me. I prefer to think of myself as a man of the world. A bon vivant, if you will. You paint me as being more of a rascal, I think."

"Bob, if you keep this thing going with Lacey, Glen will try to take you on. We both know he's no match for you in any fight, especially a gunfight. Lacey may find you dangerous and exciting, perhaps charming, but she's really in love with Glen. If you kill him or even injure him, she would never forgive you."

He gave that some thought.

"Oh, here's something else to consider—I think I may have made a huge error, and my mistake is going to make you famous."

He glanced at me in curiosity.

"I told the Bear Creek Banner the entire story of the shooting up at North Fork. I didn't think it through, and I failed to realize all of the implications.

Bob, your name and mine will be in every newspaper in the country. Everywhere you go, your name will be known. I'm sorry."

After taking a moment to absorb the news, Bob grinned.

"Ah, well, notoriety has both positive and negative implications for my business ventures. It means I will command a higher price for my services in certain capacities."

"You mean you're not upset?"

"No, I'm not, not on the whole."

"But I know you need to be able to travel without people knowing who you are."

Bob nodded.

"True, but you are no doubt aware that when I'm hunting someone, I seldom use my real name. I prefer to remain anonymous. I can still do that, as few people outside of Bear Creek have seen my face and known my name, all at the same time."

"Still, I'm sorry."

"Oh, don't trouble yourself about it. I expect being famous could have some real benefits. I imagine some of the ladies would enjoy spending some time with a famous and daring adventurer such as me. Being famous will open certain doors which might otherwise have remained closed," he winked.

I just shook my head.

***

Bob dropped me off at the house, and then he left to take the horse and buggy back to the parsonage.

I noticed the kids were not playing in the yard. I limped up the stairs and onto the porch. I looked around at the house and yard and reflected for a moment on how beautiful it was here and how nice it was to come home to peace and quiet. Once in the house, I heard noises coming from the kitchen and I could smell fresh bread baking, so I wandered in there, finding Consuela working away on supper preparations.

"Buenos tardes, Consuela. ¿Dónde está mi familia?"

"Hola, jefe. Un hombre joven condujo a la ciudad."

"¿Venga, sí? ¿Quién es el joven?"

"Es una nueva frontera. Tuvo que regresar a la ciudad para obtener sus cosas, así que conducía a la señora allí así que ella podría conseguir algunas cosas que necesito para la cena."

It seems we had a new boarder, a young man who had gone back to town to get his things and had driven my wife and the children into town to get something for Consuela at the store. It was more information than I'd asked for, but Consuela loves to talk.

"¿Cuándo espera les volver?"

"En cualquier momento ahora. Creo que él Estacione su carro aquí. ¿Qué hará con su caballo?

"I don't know where he'll put his horse. I imagine he'll put it out in the pasture with our carriage horses. If he leaves the horse and buggy at the livery stable, he'll have to walk back here." I was tired of speaking Spanish.

Consuela shrugged.

"I think you will like the stew, maybe," she said.

I went over to look in the pot, but she threatened me with a big knife.

Being easily frightened, I backed off.

"Is there any coffee?"

"Oh, sí. I mean yes, sir. Tráemelo su copa aquí."

I grabbed my favorite coffee mug, and she filled it for me. I wandered into the parlor and sat down to read the newspaper. A man came down the stairs I recognized as the other new boarder. He was the furniture and appliance salesman from Iowa, Tony Morgan.

"Howdy, Mr. Morgan, are you making any progress?"

"Good evening, Sheriff Sage. Yes. I have. Today I purchased a building lot only two blocks off the square. I'm going to build a brand new store. I'll sell furniture and appliances on the first floor. On the second floor, I'll sell housewares, linens, and sundries. The idea is to have a store right here in town where you can get everything you need for your home. I'll stock all the finest, most modern products on the market."

"That's pretty much what the general store does, isn't it?"

"The general store stocks a greater variety of items, but far fewer of them and a very limited selection. For example, the general store might have one or two sets of china dishes. I'll have half a dozen patterns to choose from. The general store will also sell shoes and candy, shotgun shells and tobacco, canned goods and kerosene. I won't be selling any of that; just things for the homemaker. The general store will show you things you can order from a catalogue. I'll have them in stock. You can buy it right here and take it home the same day. Folks won't have to allow six weeks for delivery, like they would if they bought it out of a catalog."

"It seems you've thought it through. What will you call your store?"

"It will be known as Morgan's Furniture and Appliance Emporium. It will be *the* place to get an icebox, a rug, an entire set of furniture, a wash board, a sewing machine, or all of them at the same time and in the same place."

I heard the sound of a buggy outside and figured Lora and the kids had come home.

"Well, that sounds fine, Mr. Morgan. I wish you well."

Dan Arnold

42.

When Lora and the kids came in, Lora was carrying a bag with fresh carrot tops sticking out of it. I took the bag as I kissed her. The kids giggled. I made a fierce face at them. They giggled some more.

"I have to apologize for my husband, Mr. Morgan. As you know he's the County Sheriff, and he tends to forget his manners."

Mr. Morgan didn't seem to understand how I'd displayed my bad manners. I didn't understand either.

"John, you look like you are ready to go to war. Do you really need to wear all those guns in the house?" Lora asked.

I'd taken off my hat and jacket when I came in, but I still wore my gun belt and my shoulder holster.

"No ma'am. I'll shuck out of them just as soon as I take this stuff into the kitchen."

I dropped off the bag of celery, carrots, and onions with Consuela. Lora and Consuela had used up most of what they had grown in the garden. They'd canned a bunch of produce, but preferred to use fresh vegetables whenever possible. With fall closing in, Lora's garden now had mostly just green beans, squash, and tomatoes.

In our bedroom on the ground floor, I hung my gun belt on the bed post and was about to put my shoulder holster on a hook in the wardrobe.

"John, I'd feel better if you would put your guns where the children can't reach them," Lora said from the doorway.

"Well, I like to have them close to hand. Where would you have me put them?"

"How about on top of the wardrobe; that way they'll be close to you, but out of sight and reach of the children."

I didn't like the change, but understanding her reasoning, I took my .45 out of the holster of my gun belt and put it on top of the wardrobe along with my .38 caliber Smith and Wesson pistol, still in the shoulder holster.

I spent the rest of the time before dinner playing outside with the children.

One of the things I found awkward about life at a boarding house was the constantly changing faces and the comings and goings of the guests. I had to get used to it while I had been courting Lora, and again now that we were taking in new boarders.

I'd yet to meet the newest boarder, as he'd only dropped off Lora and the kids before returning to town. He hadn't come back for supper.

Mr. Morgan had gone into town after supper to meet up with some new friends and potential business associates at the Palace.

***

After all the dishes were cleaned up and Consuela had gone home, Lora and I played with the children. As bed time approached, Lora read to them from the Bible.

She read the story about David and Goliath. The children had never heard it before and they listened with great interest. We sat and talked about what we might learn from the story. Pretty soon, Jacob and Sarah showed signs of being sleepy.

As soon as the kids were tucked into bed, Lora and I decided to do the same ourselves. We were just getting ready for bed when I heard the sound of someone coming into the house through the front door. I looked toward my guns, but Lora gave me a scowl.

"John, calm down; it's probably Mr. Wilson, the new boarder, coming in. It might even be Mr. Morgan."

I felt foolish and berated myself for being so jumpy. I was in the process of getting undressed and I'd just taken off my shirt, when Lora noticed something new.

"Oh John, is that another gunshot wound there on your neck?"

She gently reached out to touch the scabbed up area.

"It's just a crease, baby. It'll heal up quick."

"Let me see your leg," she said.

"I'll show you mine, if you'll show me yours," I replied, with a lascivious leer.

"Well, then, drop your drawers," she giggled.

I'd just done that when our bedroom door burst open.

Standing in the doorway was Homer Thorndyke, and he had a pistol in his hand.

"Well, well, I see I've caught you at a bad moment," he said.

I was standing there with my arms around Lora in her petticoat, with my pants down around my ankles. He had us covered with his gun from ten feet away. There was nothing I could do.

"Mr. Wilson!" Lora cried. "Leave here at once!"

"No, I won't be leaving. At least not for a little while. Tell her, Sheriff Sage. Tell her who I am."

I sighed.

"Lora, this is Homer Thorndyke, although I expect he introduced himself to you as someone else."

"William Wilson," she mumbled.

Homer Thorndyke stepped into the room and closed the damaged door behind him.

"Mrs. Sage, please climb up on the bed there," he said.

"I will not," she replied, clearly shaken. She was clinging to me tightly.

He looked at me.

"Tell her to do as I say, or I'll put a bullet through her head."

I ground my teeth.

Gently pushing her away from me, I said, "Go on, honey. Get up on the bed."

Lora climbed up on the bed and sat there glaring at Homer Thorndyke.

"Oh this is fun," Homer said.

Lora and I were now about five feet apart. Homer was still ten feet away from us. He had his gun pointed directly between us. He only had to move it a few inches to center on either one of us.

"Now, let's see, Sheriff Sage. Should I kill you now and then take your wife, or make you watch first, and then kill you?" Homer asked, shifting his aim back and forth.

It was a decision I'd already made.

I heard his gun thunder, and saw the flame stab at me as I leapt into him. There was no pain, but even as I reached him I knew he'd shot me. I was trying to take the gun away from him, but he was very strong and in a moment we both crashed to the floor. I was pinned under him, still trying to hang on to his gun arm with both hands.

I felt Lora brush past us and prayed she would escape.

Suddenly, he smashed his other fist into the side of my head. I saw stars.

He hit me again and again. I felt him tear his gun arm free, as I tried to clear the cobwebs from my head.

He pushed up off of me, and I was vaguely aware he stood over me bringing his gun to bear, pointed down at my head. I heard the roar of the gunshot, then another, and another. Blood splattered over me and I lost my eyesight as everything became black. I felt the weight of the world on me. It was hard to breathe. I heard myself groan.

I managed to open one eye, seeing an angel all dressed in white. She looked like Lora.

She stood there in her corset and petticoat with a gun stretched out in front of her, holding my .45 with both hands. She'd taken it down from the top of the wardrobe.

Everything was hazy.

My last thought.

"Where was Homer Thorndyke?"

43.

Life is uncertain. What we want is not always what we need. We only live one day at a time. We live today. We are not promised tomorrow.

One day each of us will give an accounting for the days we were given. Will it be today?

I thought about that accounting frequently in the following days.

***

When Bob arrived at the corner from which he liked to watch the house, he found a still smoldering cigarette butt, partially crushed on the ground. It was then he heard the first gunshot. It launched him down the hill at a dead run. The following three gunshots were ringing through the house as he flew through the front door.

He found Lora standing over the bodies of Homer Thorndyke and myself.

I was soaked in blood—his and mine, where I lay pinned under the dead man.

Lora had shot Homer Thorndyke three times. The first two shots would've ultimately proved fatal, but the last shot had been nearly point blank to the back of his head, killing him instantly.

They both thought I was dead.

Hearing the children crying, Lora started out to comfort them.

That was when I moved.

Bob hitched the team, while Lora tried to stop the bleeding, and comfort the children, all at the same time. They hauled me into town and Doc Johnson was able to save me.

Homer Thorndyke's bullet had gone right through me. Because of my leap, Thorndyke had been forced to whip his gun up and fire without aiming. The bullet entered my chest below my collarbone and exited high, out the back of my shoulder. The angle of the shot had missed my spine and any vital organs because the bullet hit a rib, breaking it and deflecting it away from my heart and lungs, but I'd lost too much blood. Doc told them it was questionable whether I would make it.

I was back on my feet by the end of the week.

***

The new preacher up at North Fork stopped by the house to see me on Thursday.

He said his name was Jeff Bradley. His right arm was in a sling, due to some injury. He and his fiancée, a lady by the name of Emma Poole, were on their way to Denver to be married.

They planned to be away until the ruckus died down.

"Your deputy has it all under control up there, John. The worst of the riff raff are already pulling out and others are changing the way they do business. North Fork will be a different town when we get back," Reverend Bradley said.

Emma nodded in agreement.

"I know you haven't been able to work out the details with the county yet, Sheriff. The house will be vacated by this weekend, and as far as I'm concerned it's available for use as an orphanage as soon as the county wants to use it. I'm prepared to deed it over with the provisions we discussed. We've decided to hold on to five acres for the church and grounds. We'll take care of all that when we get back," Emma said.

"Where will y'all live?"

"Oh, with so many people leaving, we have our choice of suitable houses, but I expect we'll build a parsonage right next to the church, at the same time the church is being built."

"I like that idea." I said.

***

On Saturday morning Tom, Becky, Lora, and I were having breakfast at our house.

Mr. Morgan had gone home, leaving us with no boarders. With no boarders about, the kids were running through the house like wild Indians.

None of us were particularly surprised when Bob came in.

He was dressed to the nines, in a brand new suit, with highly polished boots. His vest sported a gold watch chain with a fancy fob, and he had a gold stick pin in his tie. He was holding a grey derby in his left hand.

Under his suit coat, he was armed as usual, with his .45 slanted diagonally across his left hip. I caught a glimpse of a new black gun belt and holster.

He looked the perfect gentleman, otherwise.

"I just wanted to say goodbye to you folks. I'll be heading out on the 12:10 to Denver to meet with the Governor, and then I'll be off on whatever errand he has for me."

"Does Lacey know you're leaving?" Becky asked.

Bob smiled.

"Indeed she does. It seems all the celebrity caused by the newspaper stories has improved my social life. Other ladies are keeping me much too busy to spend any time with her. So, I sent her a note in which I confessed I am an unsuitable suitor, as it were. Besides, I am far too fond of my freedom to consider settling down. It seems I am by nature a tumbleweed, drifting whichever way the wind blows."

He glanced at me.

"Why, Bob, that's almost poetic," Becky said.

Tom rolled his eyes.

"And entirely true," Lora added.

I winced.

Seeing my discomfort, Bob laughed.

"Will you join us for breakfast, Bob?" Lora offered.

"I would be delighted. I was afraid you were never going to ask."

***

The only good thing about being shot was staying home, unavailable for comment or interviews by any of the host of newspaper reporters who showed up in Bear Creek in the aftermath of the violence. Some of them attempted to seek lodging with us, but Lora shooed them all away.

For a whole week now, the papers all over the country have run headlines and stories about various aspects of the shootings up at North Fork.

There are even photographs of the empty building with the signs proclaiming the place as the Gold Dust Hotel and Casino. The man with the star, seen standing in front of the building, with his gun prominently displayed, is Tommy Turner.

His story about meeting Wes Spradlin on the evening of the shootout is widely circulated.

I imagine you've seen some of the stories. Please don't believe everything you read in the papers and please don't worry, Mother.

Lora and I are both fine. We're considering adopting the children, Jacob and Sarah.

I don't know how we're going to handle all of this notoriety, or what troubles may come of it, but we'll manage somehow. If I don't get re-elected, we may be coming your way one of these days.

God only knows.

I hope all is well with you, Nick, Rachel, and the rest of the family. Lora sends her love, as do I.

Your loving son,

John

****

TURN THE PAGE FOR AN EXCERPT FROM:

RIDING FOR THE BRAND
SAGE COUNTRY Book Three

Dan Arnold

RIDING FOR THE BRAND

Sage Country Book Three

Two men on horseback stopped in the yard.

To my surprise, one of the men was "Snake" Flanagan. I'd met Snake in Amarillo. He was said to be a gunfighter, once upon a time, but we'd never had a reason to lock horns. He and I were both about fifteen years older since last we met. I hoped I'd aged better than he had. Snake had never been tall, but now he appeared thin and shrunken.

The other man was much bigger, and he appeared angry. He got off his horse and stormed up onto the porch.

"Mister, you're trespassing on private property. What're you doing here? We don't cotton to strangers nosing around." He said, looming over me.

"I have friends who used to live in this house. This is their land. I'm just having a look around. Who are you, and why are you here?" I asked.

"My name is Higgins, and this is my place now."

I shook my head.

"Not according to the deed records in the county courthouse in Bear Creek. This land belongs to the Murphy heirs."

"You're a damn liar. Who might you be, when you're at home?" Higgins asked, with a sneer.

He stood so close, his foul breath nearly knocked me over.

"My name is John Everett Sage, whether I'm at home or here on this porch."

"I don't care who you are. You leave now, or I'll dump your body in the outhouse."

I took a long slow breath. Was that what had become of Jacob and Sarah's mother? Had her body been dumped in the outhouse?

Something inside me turned to stone, and anger like a flame began spreading through me.

"Careful Higgins, he's just as likely to kill you as not," the man called 'Snake' said. "He's a dangerous gunman from way back. You may have read about him in the newspapers."

"Phaw!" spat Higgins, "Them papers tell stories so's folks will buy um. Fancy suit and all, he don't look like nothing to me."

He reached for his gun.

I was close enough to whip my gun out and smash it across his face, even as his gun came free of the holster.

Higgins crumpled, his gun was flung aside. I turned on Snake, leveling my Colt.

Snake Flanagan sat his horse calmly, and slowly lifted both hands.

"Not my fight, Sage," he grinned. "...watch your back now."

Higgins came up off the floor of the porch, quicker than I could believe. Before I could swivel fully around, he slammed into me like a run-away locomotive.

I was driven backward into a corner post of the porch. The impact knocked my gun out of my hand, the air out of my lungs, and we both crashed through the post and down into the yard.

Higgins landed on top of me, effectively keeping me from catching my breath. I was trying to shake the cobwebs out of my head and get some air, when I remembered Higgins was trying to kill me. He was a scrapper and a brawler, and he outweighed me by nearly a hundred pounds. His hands clamped around my throat, and my world began to get very small.

The sound of my hideout Colt Lightening .38 being cocked, made him stop squeezing my throat. The pressure of the barrel up under his chin made him rise up off me, as though he were being lifted by a block and tackle.

"I told you, Higgins. He's a gun slick from way back. Man like that don't kill easy." Snake observed.

There was a huge welt swelling over Higgins' right eye, from where my .45 had clipped him.

Higgins growled at Snake Flanagan, "You could've backed my play, you sum'bitch."

"I told you not to start a fight with him, you done that all on your own." Snake responded.

I pushed Higgins backward with my gun, until we reached where my .45 had landed in the yard.

I knew I would never be able to get him to Bear Creek by myself, at least not without having to kill him. He would try to jump me the first chance he got.

"You wouldn't kill an unarmed man would you?" He asked

"Higgins, you're just as dangerous with or without a gun. I expect you would have no qualms about killing me if *I* was unarmed. Now, back up over there toward your partner, so I can watch you both at the same time."

When he was far enough away, I picked up my .45, and with both guns leveled on the two men, I decided to let them go. But Higgins had something to say.

"You just bought yourself a one way ticket to hell, mister." He said.

"I don't anticipate that outcome, but I suspect *you* will most likely end up there."

"Oh, we'll meet again, alright. Maybe Jud Coltrane will let me peel your hide, and nail it to the barn door."

"Well then, maybe I should just kill you now, and save myself the trouble."

Higgins paled.

Snake said. "Whoa there, Sage, if you do, I'll have to mix in myself."

"Is that right? Are you feeling lucky, Snake? Do you think you could pull your gun faster than I can shoot both of you?"

Snake shrugged.

"It's up to you." He said.

I nodded.

"OK, Higgins this is your lucky day. Get on your horse and get out of my sight. If you try something like this again, I'll put a bullet through the pimple on your shoulders you call your head."

Higgins looked relieved, as he mounted his horse. Then he remembered something.

"What about my gun?" He asked.

"It's my gun now. Be grateful I took it, instead of your life."

Snake Flanagan had a twinkle in his eye and a little smile on his lips. He found the whole thing kind of funny.

"Thanks for staying out of this, Snake." I said.

"Por nada. When I'm ready, we'll see just how good you really are."

"...Another time, another place." I said.

"You won't have long to wait." He replied.

I watched them both ride away. When they were completely gone from sight, or sound, I holstered my .45, put my .38 back in the shoulder holster, tucked Higgins gun behind my belt, and retrieved my hat.

The yard didn't seem quite as lonely as when I had first arrived.

I walked down to the creek to get Dusty. It was time for us to go into Buttercup.

***

Dan Arnold

A note from the author

Thank you for reading Alta Vista. I would love to hear from you. You can contact me at my website ~ www.danielbanks-books.com or follow me on Goodreads~

https://www.goodreads.com/author/show/10798086.Daniel_Roland_Banks

I certainly hope you had as much fun reading this book as I had writing it. If you liked it please tell a friend - or better yet, tell the world by writing a book review on the book's page on Amazon, or on Goodreads.com.

Even a few short sentences are helpful. As an independently published author, I don't have a marketing department behind me. I only have you, the reader.

So please spread the word!

How do you write a review? It's easy.

Did you like the book? What was your favorite thing about it? Did you learn anything new or interesting? Would you like to read another book by this author? Go to the Amazon or Goodreads link, click on the "write a customer review" button and type in your review.

And, to make it a little more fun, if you write a review, e-mail me and I'll return a note and an excerpt from one of my works in progress, maybe even a free e-book.
Thanks again.

All the best,
Daniel

About the Author

I've led a colorful life, fueling my imagination for telling stories set in the American West.

I was born in Bakersfield, California and abandoned by my parents in Seattle, Washington. After living in the foster care system for some years, I was eventually adopted. I've lived in Idaho, Washington, California, Virginia, and now make my home in Texas. My wife Lora and I have four grown children, of whom we are justifiably proud, not because we were such good parents but because God is good.

I've written several novels and an illustrated book on the training of horses, in addition to authoring and/or contributing to numerous technical manuals and articles in various publications and periodicals.

As a horse trainer and clinician (I trained performance horses for twenty five years), I had occasion to travel extensively and I've been blessed to have worked with a variety of horses and people in amazing circumstances and locations.

I've herded cattle in Texas, chased kangaroos on horseback through the Australian Outback, guided pack-trips into the high Sierras and the Colorado Rockies, conditioned and trained thoroughbred race horses, galloped a warmblood on the bank of a canal surveyed by George Washington, and spent uncounted, delightful hours breaking bread with unique characters in diverse parts of the world.

At one (brief) point I was one of the 3% of fine visual artists who earned their entire income from sales of their art. I'm a painter, sculptor and writer.

Under the name Daniel Roland Banks I write contemporary detective thrillers. I'm a member of American Christian Fiction Writers and Western Writers of America.

My book ANGELS & IMPERFECTIONS was selected as finalist in the Christian Fiction category in the 2015 Reader's Favorites Book Award contest.

In 2013, after 40+ years of searching, I found and got reacquainted with my half-brother and a host of relatives from my mother's side of the family.

I can't sing or dance, but I'd like to think I'm considered an engaging public speaker, an accomplished horseman and an excellent judge of single malt Scotch.

ALTA VISTA

Dan Arnold